"Do you believe in love at first sight?"

Marcy held her breath. She had no right to ask him such a question. He was her employer, even if only temporarily, and she found him incredibly, inappropriately sexy and appealing, but she really shouldn't be so personal.

Still, she couldn't take back the question.

"I don't know," he said, his gaze direct. "I haven't experienced it myself."

Which gave her an answer in itself. He hadn't fallen for anyone at first sight, therefore he hadn't fallen for her. A stifling blanket of disappointment dropped over her.

Which was totally ridiculous, she realized. Why should she be disappointed?

"Now, lust at first sight? That's different." He took a lock of her hair in his hand and rubbed it. "It's soft. I've been wondering."

"You have?"

"Since first sight."

"Which was only—" she did some quick calculations "—seventeen hours ago."

"First sight," he repeated.

Dear Reader,

Have you ever set a goal for yourself then wouldn't deviate from it—even though you should? Being adaptable can save us a lot of grief through the years, but occasionally it takes a momentous event—like falling in love—to make us realize when we're sticking too closely to a plan.

That describes the heroine in *His Temporary Live-in Wife*. For what she believes are really good reasons, she's working toward a goal, but with blinders on, not giving herself a chance to look even side-to-side to see what else might make her happy. Along comes our hero, who's already achieved his goal and is looking for something new. He's learned to adapt.

It's up to Eric to show Marcy that it's okay to veer off course now and then, especially when the new direction could bring a greater happiness than the original path.

I cheered them on as I wrote their story. I hope you will, too.

Susan

HIS TEMPORARY LIVE-IN WIFE

SUSAN CROSBY

SPECIAL EDITION

Recycling programs
for this product may
not exist in your area.

ISBN-13: 978-0-373-65620-2

HIS TEMPORARY LIVE-IN WIFE

Copyright © 2011 by Susan Bova Crosby

www.Harlequin.com

Printed in U.S.A.

SUSAN CROSBY

believes in the value of setting goals, but also in the magic of making wishes, which often do come true—as long as she works hard enough. Along life's journey, she's done a lot of the usual things—married, had children, attended college a little later than the average coed and earned a B.A. in English. Then she dove off the deep end into a full-time writing career, a wish come true.

Susan enjoys writing about people who take a chance on love, sometimes against all odds. She loves warm, strong heroes and good-hearted, self-reliant heroines, and she will always believe in happily-ever-after.

More can be learned about her at www.susancrosby.com.

For Rob and Colleen, who live and love side by side. "Role model" may be a big, lofty title with lots of responsibility attached to it, but you've both worn it well.

Chapter One

"You want me to house-sit a vacant home? There's no furniture? Nothing?" Marcy Monroe asked her employer, bewildered. The request was a first in her four years of working for At Your Service, a Sacramento high-end temp agency. "Who hires someone to do *that?*"

"A cautious man, apparently." The agency owner, Julia Swanson, smiled in that serene way she had. "I thought since your other house-sitting job fell through, you wouldn't mind. The client will pay for a cot and sleeping bag." She handed Marcy a sheet of paper. "Here's a list of what he'll need done in the next few days. As you can see, you'll be busy. He bought it as a foreclosure, so it's not in perfect shape. The job is much more than house-sitting. He'll pay double your rate."

"Tell him to triple it and I'll do the cleaning, too," she

muttered, perusing the task list. "It'll save him having to hire a service, and it'll keep me occupied while I'm there."

Julia picked up the phone and dialed.

Marcy waved both hands, the paper flapping. "Julia, stop. I'm kidding!"

"You're kidding about offering to do the cleaning?" Julia asked.

"No, I'd do it, but—"

"Eric, hi, it's Julia Swanson.... Yes, she's sitting in my office right now. She wanted me to tell you she's willing to do the cleaning, too, for an extra fee...."

That sneaky Julia, Marcy thought. She couldn't say no now, and Julia knew it. "I don't do windows," Marcy whispered loudly.

"Of course. Here she is." Her eyes shimmering, Julia held out the phone to Marcy. "He'd like to speak with you."

Marcy shook her head at Julia but had to take the phone. "This is Marcy Monroe."

"Eric Sheridan, Ms. Monroe. Thank you very much for accepting the job. I can't tell you what a relief that is to me."

She almost sighed. It was obviously a done deal. "I'm glad I can help."

"You know the house has been vacant for months. It needs a great deal of elbow grease. Plus, it's one-and-a-half stories, with lots of windows."

Great, she thought. Just great. "That's fine."

He hesitated a beat. "Did Julia show you the list?"

"Yes, and I don't foresee any problems, Mr. Sheridan. You can relax. I'm quite competent."

"I was already promised that. I'm leaving New York

City today to drive across the country. Feel free to call me anytime you have questions. I'd rather not be surprised when I get there."

"I will, thanks."

"If you would put Julia back on, please?"

Marcy passed her the phone and watched Julia laugh at something the man said. He'd been all business with *her*. Marcy couldn't imagine what was so funny—unless it had to do with her somehow.

After a few seconds, Julia hung up. "He said to hire a window-cleaning service."

Marcy felt her face heat. "He heard me say that?"

"Apparently. Or he's clairvoyant."

"What does he do?"

"He'll be teaching mathematics for the fall quarter at UC Davis starting next month."

A mathematician—which probably meant he was a stickler for details and more pragmatic than fun. She'd met several in her past life as a flight attendant. "I'll only be dealing with him, no one else?"

"Right." Julia leaned forward. "I know you feel trapped into accepting the job, Marcy, but if you're really not interested, you can back out."

"No, I'll do it. It's just so weird staying in an empty house, you know? Kind of creepy."

"Invite a friend to stay overnight with you, if you want." She passed Marcy an envelope. "Here's the key and some cash for supplies. The utilities have been turned on. Thank you so much for doing this. I think he could end up being a long-time client for other occasions."

Marcy said goodbye then took the stairs down three flights from the downtown Sacramento office. Julia's business was often nicknamed "Wives for Hire" because of jobs like this one.

Marcy decided to check out the client's house before shopping for supplies, so she headed for the town of Davis, a half hour's drive from Sacramento. She pulled up in front of a quaint Craftsman-style home with wood-shake siding, rock pillars and a wraparound porch, a masculine-looking structure. That was the upside.

The downside was a lawn and landscaping that had died for lack of watering during however long it had been in foreclosure.

And the windows? She counted twenty-four just on the front.

She stepped out of the car, the late August heat hitting her squarely in the face. Today marked the seventh day in a row the temperature had reached one hundred, although the stately old trees that lined the block provided good shade. It was an old, established neighborhood of well-maintained, decades-old houses, the kind of place where kids could play in the street without too much worry.

Grateful she didn't have to wash the multitude of windows, Marcy was smiling as she opened the front door and stepped inside a wide living room that looked as if it had been a frat house once. Everything needed painting. Walls needed repair. The floors were dirty, but seemed to have weathered the storm well enough.

Like most Craftsman houses, it wasn't open-concept, but separate rooms. In the dining room she discovered a broken window with glass scattered across the floor, and footprints—human and animal—in the accumulated dust. The half bath was filthy. So was the kitchen.

The cabinets were usable but the appliances and countertops old and in need of replacement. Upstairs were three bedrooms and two bathrooms, one within the master suite that must have been renovated sometime in the past twenty years. Overhead light fixtures had been ripped out, and although the walls weren't badly damaged, they needed paint.

The house would sparkle like a gem when it was clean and fixed up, but it was going to take a lot of effort to get it to that point.

She regretted telling the owner she would do the cleaning. It was a much bigger job than she'd expected.

Marcy glanced at the to-do list. Painters were to arrive starting the next day. An interior designer was on the schedule. The moving van was due on Friday, four days from now. Mr. Sheridan hoped to arrive on Saturday, perhaps Sunday.

Marcy wandered into the backyard, which had a covered deck and built-in barbecue that had somehow survived with only a little weather-related damage. The lot wasn't overly large, and the neighbors fairly close, but a fence surrounded the property as well as enough greenery to maintain some privacy.

Someone on a bicycle came barreling down the driveway, a teenage boy, maybe sixteen or seventeen years old.

"Hi," he said, getting off his bike but holding on to it. "I'm Dylan. I saw the For Sale was taken down. Are you the new owner? 'Cause I'm looking for work, and this place could use it. I know I don't look it, but I'm strong."

There was a desperateness about him that drew her

sympathy. He was rib-showing skinny, and his hair hadn't been cut in a while.

"I'm sorry, Dylan. I don't have any authority to hire anyone. Maybe if you come back next week?"

More than disappointment crossed his face. Despair? Hopelessness?

She dug into her pocket, pulled out a twenty-dollar bill and tucked it into his hand. "Come back next week, okay?"

He didn't debate about taking the money, which told her a lot. He mumbled his thanks then took off.

She watched him until he was out of sight, then walked the perimeter, checking out the neglected yard. She returned to the house to make a list before calling the new owner.

"Mr. Sheridan, this is Marcy Monroe. I'm at your house. When was the last time you saw it?"

"Call me Eric, please. I saw it three months ago, why?"

"There's damage in almost every room." She told him what she'd found. "Was the house in that condition when you saw it?"

"No." Annoyance coated the single word.

"We should postpone the painters until the walls are fixed, don't you think? I know it's going to throw your schedule off, but I don't see that you have a choice."

He blew out a breath. "My Realtor didn't tell me. She should have."

"Maybe she didn't know. It's hard to tell when it happened. I think the first priority is to fix the broken window. And honestly, I don't want to stay here until I know it's secure."

"I believe an occupied house will scare off vagrants

and prevent more damage from occurring, which is why I asked for someone to spend the night."

"But—"

"But I agree about the window," he said, interrupting her before she got started on her argument. "Go ahead and have that fixed, today if possible. Offer a bonus, if necessary. After that, I'd like you to stay at night, as planned. Unless you don't want the job now?"

She was tempted to back out, but she prided herself on her reliability. She'd agreed to the job. She would stick it out. Plus, the work involved a whole lot of money, and she wouldn't turn that down. It would help make up for losing out on the two-week house-sitting job she'd counted on.

"I'm not quitting," she said. "Actually, I'm used to sleeping in strange houses, although not unfurnished ones. I also wondered if you want me to buy a vacuum cleaner."

"I have one, but it's in the moving van. Doesn't do much good there, does it?"

"I can borrow one. I should get going. There's a lot to do."

"I appreciate your checking with me."

She pushed the end button and stared at her phone. He had a pleasant voice. More than that, really—an enticing voice, deep and clear, although a somewhat-formal tone. She didn't think students would have any trouble listening to him lecture.

She should've asked Julia how old he was. She had no visual image of him. He sounded settled. Professorial. She pictured a man in his sixties, wearing a sweater vest and tweed jacket with elbow patches.

Marcy smiled at the stereotype that formed in her

head. She wasn't anywhere near settled, but twenty-eight and still working toward her educational goals, and then to a career to sustain her through good times and bad.

Her future was something she could ponder forever, but for now she had a job to do—get the window fixed so she could spend her first night in the cave Eric Sheridan called home.

Eric made a final walk-through of his empty co-op. Having some last-minute business to tend to before he could leave town, he'd been staying at a hotel since the movers had packed everything a few days earlier. In a few minutes he would hit the road. He could've flown, could've had the car moved with his belongings, but had decided he needed to clear his head so that he could start fresh in California. A road trip would do that.

He needed to let go of his life in New York City. A year had gone by since Jamie had been taken from him, and Eric was still stuck in the anger stage of mourning, one he was well familiar with, unfortunately. This time he knew he had to find a way to make quicker work of the other grief stages and get on with life. He'd been offered a teaching position at MIT, his alma mater and where his father had taught for many years, as well. But a move to the west coast seemed...cleaner.

He was almost forty, and he was done with the singles scene. He wanted to live near family, not just gather with them for holidays. His brothers were scattered around the country, but his sister lived just north of Sacramento. She was newly married and not bound to leave the area anytime soon.

More important, he wanted marriage and children,

and had bought a house suitable for raising a family. He'd been waiting for years to settle down, fulfilling his many other responsibilities before seeing to his own needs. He'd raised his four siblings after their parents died, and he didn't regret or resent what he'd done, but it was his time now.

His cell phone rang, jarring him out of his reverie. He saw it was Marcy Malone again. "Yes, Marcy?"

"I hope I'm not interrupting anything."

"I'm in my empty apartment, making a final pass-through. What can I do for you?"

"I wanted to let you know that the window has been fixed."

"Good."

"However," she added, "I just realized there are no blinds or curtains. Not a one."

"I'm aware of that."

"Have you ordered some? I don't see anything on the list about it."

The nerves he'd heard in their previous conversation seemed more intense now. "The interior designer is handling it. I take it you're afraid to stay there without window coverings?"

There was a long pause, as if she was weighing her words and being careful not to displease the client. "I'm okay," she said finally but in a tone that seemed to indicate she was trying to convince herself.

He should've asked Julia Swanson for information on Marcy Malone. He'd like a visual to put to the voice. She sounded young. "If you're sure," he said, not wanting to have her replaced, but also not wanting her to fear staying in the house alone.

"I'm sure. Okay, then. That's all I wanted to know."

"I'm glad you called," he said. "Don't hesitate, no matter how trivial the issue seems."

"Thanks. Have a safe trip."

He said good-night then wandered to the living-room window, which overlooked Central Park. He'd taken Jamie there. They'd rollerbladed, eaten ice cream and talked a lot—about life and expectations and what mattered most.

His time with Jamie had given Eric insight into the kind of life he wanted. A wife who was calm and soothing, but stable and competent, too. Maternal. Especially maternal.

And willing to put her career on hold until their children were raised, a hopelessly chauvinistic and politically incorrect demand, but he wasn't an idealistic young man any more. He knew what he wanted, what he could live with, and what were deal breakers. He wouldn't settle. He'd earned the right to pursue his own happiness after all he'd been through.

Eric locked the door of his co-op for the last time. Anticipation lightened his step, the same level of excitement he'd felt when his Realtor first took him into the house he'd ended up buying. The feeling was rare for him, and welcome.

He hoped it was a sign of more to come.

By the third day of his drive, Eric had gotten antsy. Talk radio couldn't hold his attention, music only annoyed him. He'd downloaded an audio book, a thriller that should've dug its suspenseful claws into him and made the time pass quickly. It didn't work.

Why had he ever thought that driving across the country was a good way to transition to his new life?

He was miserable. He talked on his cell phone to his siblings, old friends, and a few business acquaintances until they made up excuses to get off the phone.

The only one who didn't offer an excuse and rush off was Marcy Monroe, but he was also paying her for her time. He'd come to enjoy his conversations with her a lot.

His phone rang. Speak of the devil, he thought, smiling. "Hello, Marcy."

"Hi. How's it going?"

"I just passed through Lincoln, Nebraska. I found a great hamburger place on the outskirts of the city. What's up?"

"The installers are here with your washer and dryer. I just wanted to double-check that you ordered Zephyr Blue?"

She said it with such doubt in her voice, he grinned. "That's the color."

"Okay. Let me tell them. Hold on a sec. Yes, that's fine. Go ahead," she said to the installers.

"I guess you can't picture me with Zephyr Blue appliances," he commented.

"It's weird because I'm doing all this personal work for you but I don't know anything beyond the fact you're a math professor. May I ask why you're moving here?"

"For the women."

"I beg your pardon?"

He laughed. "I'm looking to get married and have children. I've exhausted New York."

Her response was a little slow in coming. "I know a lot of women. What are you looking for?"

"Do you? Because I don't want to do the whole online dating thing, so a personal reference would be great.

She has to want kids, even though this would be my second family. I've already raised four to adulthood."

"Four?" she repeated, a little breathlessly. "Ah, what age are you looking for?"

"She needs to be childbearing age, of course, but not too young. I'm not looking to rob any cradles."

"So, you're divorced? Or widowed?"

"Neither."

"You're a single dad?"

Eric was having way too much fun with her, but he didn't want to explain everything and turn the conversation serious. He was tired of serious. It was one of his reasons for making the move. "It's a long story," he said.

"May I ask you this—did they all have the same mother?"

"Absolutely."

Dead silence followed. "I hope you'll share the story sometime," she said finally.

"That's a date."

"Good. In the meantime, I'll look through my address book and see if I can come up with some names."

"That is above and beyond the call of duty, Marcy. Thank you."

Eric started whistling after they hung up, then he found music on the satellite radio that he could sing along with. He was beginning to feel more than a little hopeful about his fresh start. He even had a matchmaker willing to help.

He rolled down his window and flew down the Interstate singing at the top of his lungs. He couldn't wait to get to California and see who she had in mind.

Chapter Two

Early Friday morning, Marcy dragged herself out of her sleeping bag and stumbled into the bathroom to splash cold water on her face. She stared at her haggard reflection.

"One more night to go," she reminded herself. It had been a very long week, but Eric was making good time on the road and thought he would arrive sometime tomorrow afternoon. In some ways she was ready to move on, but since her house-sitting job had been canceled, she didn't have anywhere to go the following week. Usually she stayed at her back-up home, her friend Lori's apartment, but she had out-of-town company, leaving no room for Marcy. She'd checked with two other friends, but they both had live-in boyfriends, a surprise to her, so that wouldn't work.

For the first time in ages, she would have to get a motel room.

But whichever way it worked out, a full night's sleep was in sight for her, for which she was grateful. Eric's house made noise all night, sounds she couldn't identify, creaks and groans and clunks. Tree branches scraped against windows. A couple of times she thought she'd heard footsteps, but in the morning there were no signs of anyone having been inside.

She knew she was being ridiculous. Paranoid, probably. In her sane moments, she chalked it up to being in an empty building. Furniture, drapes and carpets absorbed sound, but empty houses echoed, magnifying even a hum into a clatter.

She'd placed her cot and sleeping bag against the locked bedroom door, and had never gotten out of bed to check out a noise.

One more night...

After the quickest shower on record, Marcy opened the bedroom door a crack and peeked out. She listened. A minute later she left the room and tiptoed downstairs, going from room to room, finding nothing out of place. Daylight vanquished ghosts and lessened fears. She'd relaxed by the time she opened the refrigerator. She'd already stocked it with the items on Eric's list but had bought things for herself, too, like individual-size bottles of orange juice. She grabbed one, then noticed it was the last.

She'd bought five bottles. This was day four.

Marcy moved food around, not finding another bottle. Had one of the workmen taken one?

She searched a little more but didn't notice anything else missing. From a cabinet she grabbed a loaf of bread and jar of peanut butter, at least a half of which was missing. She'd only made one sandwich.

Marcy dropped the jar to the counter. Half the loaf of bread was gone, too. It wasn't her imagination.

She shoved both items into a grocery bag then washed her hands. Who could've taken the food? What else had they handled? It had to be someone who'd been in the house during the past two days. Who had she left unsupervised?

The drywall repairer had worked on Tuesday and part of yesterday, so it could have been him. And she'd left him alone when the washer and dryer were delivered yesterday. But the laundry room was just off the kitchen, so she would've seen him sneak into the kitchen. Several boxes of window treatments had arrived later in the day. The deliveryman hadn't gone beyond the living room.

That left the painters. No one else had been in the house for long.

What could she do about it? She could call and complain to their boss, but anyone bold enough to steal would also lie. She had no proof, either. Now she would have to do an inventory and replace whatever else was missing.

Plus deal with the creepiness of the whole thing.

She carried the trash outside to put in the bin, but the bin was gone. Two bins, actually, trash *and* recycling. Then she noticed that the old drywall the workman had tossed outside was also gone.

Marcy followed the driveway to the front yard and spotted the bins. Next to them were the appliance cartons, broken down and stacked on the sidewalk, ready to be picked up. The trash container was filled with drywall scraps.

"We have so much trash today, don't we, Lucy?" a woman said nearby.

Marcy saw the next-door neighbor try to muscle her trash bin to the curb and carry a toddler at the same time. Marcy rushed over.

"May I help?" she asked.

"Thank you." She followed Marcy to the sidewalk. "Are you my new neighbor?"

"No, I'm just helping to get the house in order before the owner comes." She put out her hand. "My name's Marcy."

"I'm Annie and this is Lucy. She's two. Say hi, Luce." The woman was tall and slender, probably in her early thirties, with straight blond hair to her shoulders. And no wedding ring.

The little girl lowered her chin but looked up flirtatiously, making Marcy laugh. "It's very nice to meet you, Lucy, and Lucy's mommy."

"We've been looking forward to having the house occupied." She glanced toward it. Her own place was more Victorian in design, as true to the era as Eric's.

"I would feel the same. By any chance, did you haul my trash to the street? I got up this morning and found it done."

"Wasn't me, but we've got a block full of helpful neighbors. You'll probably find out who did it sometime today. We'll, we're on our way to mommy-and-me swim class. I'll talk to you later."

Check, check, check, Marcy thought. Annie might be slightly on the young side, but she was the best candidate so far for Eric. Marcy would try to get more info on her later today. Of course, being next-door neighbors could be too complicated, especially if they dated then it didn't work out.

When Marcy got back to the kitchen she stopped and stared. She hadn't noticed earlier that the dishes had been done. There hadn't been many, but the counter was clean. It shouldn't have been.

Which meant someone had been inside the house. During the night. While she slept.

The doorbell rang, heralding the arrival of the window washers, who planned to be there for hours, as would the painters, finishing up two upstairs rooms. She welcomed the distraction. The moving company had called yesterday to say she could expect the van to arrive around ten. Marcy had contacted the interior designer, passing along that news.

Everyone should be gone by the time she headed to her regular weekend waitress job. Even being on her feet all night would seem like a vacation after this week.

On the other hand, her checkbook was going to be very happy, especially her tuition fund.

A couple hours later, one of the window washers pointed out a broken lock on a dining room window, not the one she'd had repaired, but the window next to it. She'd never noticed. It appeared locked, but actually wasn't latching into anything, a section of the latch having been broken or cut away. The window slid up and down with little effort.

One more item for her to-do list. One more thing to worry about on her last day and night.

She examined the dining-room floor, looking for evidence that someone had broken in. Since she'd been watering the yard every day, it was muddy outside the window now. Anyone who climbed through the window would've had mud on their shoes. She found nothing, however.

How could she possibly come back here after her shift tonight? It would be well past midnight, and the house dark and empty, and easy to break into. Apparently *had* already been broken into. Would Eric be angry if she didn't spend the night?

Probably, especially now that his personal belongings would be delivered.

Okay then. She would just have to stay awake. She had a cell phone and a can of pepper spray.

She could handle anything.

Eric had come to appreciate his GPS more than ever on his trip across America. Not only did he know where he was going and how to get there, he also easily found hotels, gas stations and restaurants.

But also because of the unit's efficiency, he knew exactly how many hours of driving he had ahead of him. Which tonight prompted a big decision. It was ten o'clock. He was three hours out of Davis, California, his ultimate destination. He'd been on the road most of the day. Usually by now he was settled into a hotel room and asleep.

It's only three hours. You could sleep in your own bed tonight.

But could he stay awake? Was it worth the exhaustion?

Yes. He would be home. He would be too restless if he went to a hotel now, anyway.

He dialed Marcy's phone but only reached her voice mail. Maybe she'd already gone to bed. She'd had a long, busy day, he knew.

"Marcy, it's Eric," he said. "I just wanted to alert you that I'll be arriving around 1:00 a.m. Didn't want to catch you by surprise. When you get this message, please call me back. Thanks."

A little under three hours later, he pulled into his driveway and parked in front of his detached garage, assuming Marcy's car was inside it. The house was dark. She hadn't returned his call, so he figured she was asleep.

Hesitant about giving her a shock, he approached the front door quietly, key in hand. He checked his phone in case she'd called back and he hadn't heard it ring, but there weren't any messages.

Should he call her again now, before he went inside, so that if she woke up she wouldn't think he was an intruder? What if she kept a gun for protection?

He dialed, figuring it was better to startle her out of sleep than come face-to-face with her. They'd never seen each other. She could scream, wake the neighbors, get the police involved....

Still no answer. He hung up without leaving a message.

He slid his key into the lock, opened the door slowly. He didn't turn on any lights, a streetlamp in front of his house and his porch light offering enough illumination to see where he was going.

His furniture was in place but boxes were stacked to one side. He walked down the hall and into the dining room, stopping cold when he saw one window partially open.

She'd gone to bed with the window open? What an idiotic—

A slight noise reached him. He spun around. Some-one was nearby. Marcy? No, she wouldn't tiptoe....

Was she all right?

He rushed from the room and down the hall in time to see someone reach the front door. Eric picked up speed. The person flung open the door and ran out... and crashed into someone—Marcy, Eric decided, hearing a woman yelp. Knocked to the ground, she'd slowed the intruder's escape long enough for Eric to grab him and slam him against the side of the house, driving his shoulder into him to prevent him from going anywhere. A kid, Eric thought. A teenager, maybe only seventeen.

"Eric?" Marcy asked breathlessly, warily. She stood up and backed off at the same time. She was looking at him as if he was the bad guy.

The kid tried to wriggle away. Eric pushed him harder into the siding and grunted. "Yes, I'm Eric," he said to Marcy, who looked nothing like he'd expected. He'd imagined her as young and petite. She was close to thirty, he decided, above average in height, with generous curves and long, wild, auburn hair.

She smiled a little, shaky but sassy, too. "Welcome to California." She pointed at the boy. "That's Dylan. He's looking for work."

"You know him? You invited him to stay in my house without asking me?"

"Of course not. I have no idea how he got inside."

"Through the window you left open," Eric said.

She frowned. "What window?"

"In the dining room. Wide open."

"I didn't, I promise you. The lock—"

"Let's take this inside." He would deal with her incompetence later. He didn't want his new neighbors observing this scene as their introduction.

Eric maneuvered the teenager into the living room and onto a chair then stood over him. Marcy followed, turning on lights. The boy was tall and skinny, with dirty brown hair and eyes teeming with belligerence.

Great, Eric thought. *Just what I needed tonight.*

"Do you want me to call the police?" Marcy asked, leaning against the front door.

"Not yet. So. Dylan what?" Eric asked the kid.

He glared back silently.

"You're telling me or you're telling the cops. Which is it?"

A flash of hope sprang in his eyes. Eric had already come to some conclusions about him.

The boy remained silent. Eric reached for his cell phone.

"Anthony," Dylan said in a rush.

Eric wondered if that was really his name. "How old are you?"

"Eighteen."

"Prove it."

"I can't."

"Where do you live?"

"Nowhere. Everywhere. Here, for a while. It got complicated once she—" he jerked his head toward Marcy "—moved in."

"You ate my peanut butter," she said.

He lifted his chin, gave her a dark look. "You don't look like you've missed any meals."

"Knock it off," Eric said. "You want to save your hide, be respectful."

Dylan looked at the floor.

"I gave you money, and this is how you repay me?" Marcy asked.

"I didn't ask you for anything except a job, lady. And I did stuff— Never mind."

"Are you hungry?" Eric asked, knowing the answer. They could sort this out when everyone calmed down.

"Wait," Marcy said. "You did what stuff?" she asked Dylan. "Finish your sentence."

He shrugged.

"It was *you*. You broke down the boxes and put them out for recycling. You put the trash out so the drywall could be hauled off. You even did the dishes!"

After a few seconds he nodded, not making eye contact.

Apparently there was a lot more to this kid than appeared on the surface. He hadn't just stolen. "Marcy, would you please fix Dylan a sandwich or something," Eric said. "Whatever you've got on hand."

She sighed. "Would you also like one?"

"If you don't mind."

"Oh, no. I'm here to serve," she muttered as she strode into the kitchen, although "marched" might be a more accurate description.

Eric pulled a chair close to Dylan and sat. "Tell me about living here. How'd you do that?"

"Opened the window. Climbed in."

Eric dug for patience. "Be more specific."

"I saw the place was empty. I needed a place to stay."

"Did you break the window?"

"It was already broken." He finally made eye contact, although only briefly. "I broke the lock on the other window so I could get back in, in case someone fixed the glass."

"How long did you stay here?"

He shrugged.

"Days? Weeks? Months?"

"When I needed to."

Eric waited, his gaze steady. Silence usually brought discomfort and therefore answers, but this kid handled empty silences well.

"Go wash your hands before we eat." He reckoned the boy was hungry enough not to climb out the window. "I think you know where the bathroom is."

Dylan had perfected the teenage saunter. He didn't act scared or nervous, but Eric figured he was plenty of both.

Eric joined Marcy in the kitchen, planting himself where he could see if Dylan tried to escape. She glanced at Eric then returned to fixing what looked to be turkey sandwiches and chips.

"The boy's cleaning up," he said.

"I could hear your conversation."

"Need help?"

"No, thanks."

She went silent but he noted how stiff-backed she was. "You don't approve of me not phoning the police."

"At first I thought you should, but now that I know he's been my secret helper, I'd be more hesitant to turn him in. He seems desperate, and not all bad."

"Don't be too quick to make that kind of decision. He's no innocent."

"He's no hardened criminal, either."

Her hair had fallen along the side of her face, hiding her expression, but also giving him a moment for a longer glimpse of her.

Dylan's comment about her not looking as if she missed meals wasn't accurate. She was just curvy, very curvy, top and bottom, but with a small waist, proportionately. A perfect hourglass. She wore a low-cut T-shirt with the word "Score" blazoned across it, and skin-tight jeans. Too many questions came to mind. He was trying not to jump to conclusions as much as he had in the past.

"Where were you tonight?" he asked.

"I wait tables at a sports bar on Friday and Saturday nights." She faced him. "I didn't know the window lock was broken until today when the window washer pointed it out. As you'll see for yourself, it's not immediately evident. I made arrangements for it to be repaired, but the guy couldn't come until tomorrow. Today."

"You should've offered a bonus to come today. If you'd called me about it, I would've told you to do that. You should know that about me by now."

"Apparently money solves all your problems," she murmured.

Annoyed at her tone, he came up beside her so that Dylan wouldn't overhear any more of their conversation. "Most of the time, yes. You didn't turn down the extra pay I offered."

"True." After a minute, she said, "What are you going to do about him?"

"I haven't decided, but he needs to learn there are consequences for his actions."

Dylan stepped into the room then. He swallowed as

he eyed the sandwiches. He also looked ready to take flight.

"I know all about consequences," Dylan said, looking as if the world was one big heavy weight on his shoulders.

Eric saw Marcy become a puddle of sympathy. He figured the kid had learned survival techniques, one of them being to figure out who might be the softest touch. He would probably zero in on Marcy now, because she'd played her hand already. He knew she cared about what happened to him.

"What would you like to drink?" she asked.

"Milk. If you've got it."

"I think by now you know what she's got," Eric said. "You're not eating?" he asked Marcy as she passed their plates to them.

"I ate at work."

His long day of driving, followed by all he'd been met with here, combined to deliver him a one-two punch of exhaustion. He wasn't even hungry anymore. He just needed sleep. And no problems to deal with for at least ten hours.

So much for starting fresh somewhere else. Welcome to California, indeed.

"You can sleep in the living room," he said to Dylan, deciding that if he hadn't taken anything other than food the last five days, he wasn't likely to do so now. "I expect you to be here when I get up in the morning, even if that's not until noon."

Dylan said nothing. He just ate, taking big bites, devouring the sandwich.

Eric glanced at Marcy when Dylan refused to answer.

"What? You plan on ordering me, too?" she asked, challenge and humor in her eyes.

"Where have you been sleeping?"

"On a cot in your bedroom. Your furniture was set up today, and your bed is made, by the way. I'll just move into one of the spare bedrooms for the night. I'm sure we'll have business to discuss in the morning. Good night."

She was a lot more lively in person than on the phone, and she wasn't acting much like an employee. Not that he minded, except that his perceptions of her were all wrong, and that usually wasn't the case.

He watched Dylan eat. Eric had seen what could happen to teenagers on the streets of New York. Things might not be as dire in the university town of Davis, but everyone deserved better than being reduced to scrounge for food and shelter. And everyone he knew who'd gotten involved with a homeless person had gotten bitten in some way.

He wanted to trust his instincts about the kid, but he knew he should keep his guard up. "Want another sandwich?" he asked.

"She made chocolate-chip cookies today, but I'm guessing they're for you," Dylan said, pointing to a plastic container on the counter.

Eric leaned back in his chair, grabbed it and set it in front of the boy. Dylan didn't hesitate. He yanked the top off and pulled out a handful. Eric went to the refrigerator to get the milk again, deciding to give up asking questions. The kid would talk when he was ready.

After a few minutes Marcy materialized in the doorway. "I made up a bed for Dylan on the sofa," she said, then disappeared as quickly and quietly as she'd come.

They rinsed their plates in the kitchen sink then walked into the living room. The sofa looked welcoming. Because it was a normal hot August night, she hadn't added a blanket, only sheets, but she'd turned down the top sheet invitingly and put a chocolate mint on his pillow.

Eric smiled at that. She may not trust Dylan being there, and she may even harbor resentment for his sneaking into the house under her watch, but she still recognized he could use a little comfort.

"Are you gonna call the cops?" Dylan asked, scuffing his toe against the hardwood floor.

He was too tired to deal with it. "We'll talk about it in the morning." He dragged his hands down his face.

Dylan sprang into action, making a quick side step around Eric, running to the door. He was already to the front sidewalk by the time Eric made it to the porch.

He should've anticipated that, but he'd figured Dylan would be grateful for the food and the offer of a place to sleep, although Eric had fully expected him to leave before sunrise.

Eric locked the door, then climbed the stairs. He could probably find something to wedge into the window jam, making it impossible to open, but he didn't bother. If Dylan changed his mind, he would have a way in.

When Eric reached the second floor, he didn't see a light on under either guest-room door, so he didn't know which room she'd taken. His bedroom door was open, however, and a lamp on. He stepped over the threshold. His quilt was folded at the foot of the bed, leaving only sheets for him, too. The house was warm even with the air conditioner on.

And there was a mint on his pillow.

Even though she was wary of having Dylan in the house, and had borne the brunt of his own anger for the window lock not being fixed, she'd turned his room into a retreat for him.

He dug out shorts and a T-shirt from his suitcase and climbed into bed. The sheets felt crisp and smelled fresh, as did his room. He'd had housecleaners all his adult life, but that's all they did—clean house.

Marcy had already made him a home.

Chapter Three

Marcy jolted straight up in bed when the doorbell rang, followed by someone pounding on the door. She flung back the covers, grabbed her cell phone to check the time—3:30 a.m.—then rushed out of the bedroom, pulling on a summer-weight robe.

From the top of the staircase Marcy saw Eric open the front door. Two uniformed officers stood there, Dylan in front of them, looking hostile.

"We caught him as he dropped out a window out back," one officer said. "Neighbor phoned it in that she'd seen someone climb inside. He was carrying this." He held up the plastic container of cookies Marcy had baked. "Says he knows you."

"We've met," Eric said, his arms crossed, his eyes drilling the boy.

"You want to press charges?" the cop asked.

"I don't know. Do I want to press charges, Dylan?"

Marcy saw the boy's hostility transform into fear. Scared, he looked even younger.

"It's just cookies," he muttered.

"And breaking and entering," Eric pointed out.

"The window wasn't locked," Dylan said, cockiness not just in his voice but his stance.

The look Eric gave him would've reduced Marcy to a quivering mass, but Dylan challenged him right back with his eyes.

The look might not have backed Dylan down but he did respond to it. His hostile expression smoothed out, and he stood a little taller, waiting for a verdict.

"Charges, sir?" the now-impatient officer asked.

"No. Let him go." Eric started to shut the door.

"Wait! Give him the cookies," Dylan ordered the cop. "I'm sorry."

Marcy watched Eric close his eyes for a few seconds and then assume the stern-parent look before he re-opened the door. The officer passed Eric the container. He and his partner strode off.

"I'll be right back. Don't move," Eric said to Dylan as he stood on the porch, then Eric caught up with the police officers, entering into a discussion for a couple of minutes before returning. He walked past Dylan, went inside, then turned at the threshold. "Do you have anything to say?"

"I know I was stupid to do that," Dylan said right away.

"You think?"

"I've been on my own awhile. I'm not used to some-one being nice to me."

"Cut the crap," Eric said, shocking Marcy. Dylan had seemed genuinely sorry.

"Maybe that works on some people, but not me. There's no reason for someone your age to be homeless, not with all the public options available. You've chosen to be. I don't know if you're running or hiding, but I expect other people have been *nice* to you." Eric leaned close to him. "You've heard of the three-strikes law?"

Dylan nodded.

"You've got two in my book. Good night." He shut the door in the boy's face.

Marcy's heart caught in her throat. He was just a kid, a scared kid. "You're sending him out there again? In the middle of the night?"

His face looked cold, so very cold. "Coddling is not going to help this boy, even though he could use a whole lot of that, too. If he wants help, he'll knock. He needs to be a man. Someone hasn't taught him that."

"But you will?"

"I don't see anyone else stepping up, do you? But he has to want it. Look, those cops already knew him. I told them we were thinking about letting him stay with us, so they were straight with me. He had some trouble at one of the shelters and got booted out, but the cops think it wasn't his fault. He hasn't gotten into any trouble that they know of. Keeps his head down and his nose clean. That's high praise in my mind. They gave me a couple of people to check with. That and my own gut feeling says we can let him stay here for now."

A quiet knock came on the door.

Eric didn't make him wait long before he pulled open the door.

"I'm sorry."

"For what?" Eric asked.

He drew a shaky breath. "Breaking in. Taking the cookies. Not being cool after you tried to help me."

"Apology accepted."

They faced off, one more question hanging between them. Dylan gave in first. "I'd like to stay the night, if the offer's still good."

"It's good." Eric backed away, letting him in. "Don't do anything that deprives me of sleep for the next six hours or so." He passed Dylan the cookies then headed up the staircase without looking back.

Marcy resisted the temptation to hover over the boy, even though the look on his face just about broke her heart. "You know where the milk is," she said. "Good night, Dylan."

"Night." His voice was tight, as if he was fighting tears.

She touched his arm. "You'll be all right," she said, her throat burning, her heart aching. He wasn't a hardened criminal but a kid who'd somehow lost his way. "Mr. Sheridan seems like the right person to trust," she added.

He nodded. She patted his arm instead of hugging him, as she was tempted to do, then she climbed the stairs and got into bed.

Sleep eluded her. So much had happened in the past few hours that it seemed like a whole day. Taking center stage in her thoughts was what a surprise Eric had been. She'd expected a man decades older, but she doubted he was forty. He was at least six feet tall, and his temples were graying, but otherwise his hair was light brown, cut not so short as to look severe but not long enough to fall into his face. His eyes were a deep, rich, penetrating brown. And he was built like a football player, sturdy and solid. Sexy, actually. Strong, too. He'd dealt with Dylan on the porch earlier swiftly and powerfully but without hurting him.

Eric didn't seem to have much of a sense of humor, but he hadn't exactly walked into a situation allowing or requiring one—and he was a mathematician, after all. He was probably logical to a fault. At the moment he must be wondering about his decision to move to Davis, especially now that he seemed fated to become responsible for a stray with criminal tendencies.

Marcy smiled at the ceiling. She was a big believer in fate, which had led her down some interesting paths in life. And she couldn't shake the feeling that fate had just dealt her the most important hand of her life when her last-two-weeks-of-August, regular-as-clockwork, house-sitting job had fallen through for the first time in four years, leaving her free to take this job.

She had nowhere to go tomorrow, and she felt a strong draw to the man in this crazy scenario. Would he ask her to stay? Would he be her hero?

She didn't usually have such fantasies. She had goals to accomplish, after all, and promises to keep—with no time to slack off, not even when it involved a gorgeous math professor who summed up a situation and took control immediately and well. And who made her heart flutter with just a look.

Nope. No time for that at all. It was better if he didn't need her to stay. Safer.

But then safer wasn't always better, was it?

* * *

The next morning, Marcy lay in bed listening. It was almost 10:00 a.m., but she hadn't heard any sounds of movement in the few minutes she'd been awake. She wondered if Dylan was still asleep or had flown the coop. Or cleaned out the refrigerator.

She'd slept well, having relinquished responsibility to Eric.

Prepared for another hundred-degree day, Marcy pulled on shorts and a tank top, then left her room. Eric's bedroom door was closed. She slipped into the guest bath, cleaned up, and made her way downstairs.

The sofa was empty, although the sheets were jumbled, so Dylan had slept there at some point.

Disappointment washed over her. She'd hoped not only that the boy would realize Eric would probably continue to help him, but also that Dylan would prove himself worthy of Eric's trust.

She heard the shower in the master bath come on and headed for the kitchen. She would fix a nice breakfast before she left, wanting to end the job on good terms. She was curious, too, about his reaction to Dylan being gone.

She fixed cheese omelets and wheat toast, filled a bowl with grapes and cantaloupe. She was just about to slide the plates into a warm oven when she heard the creak of the stairs as Eric made his way down. He didn't pause but came directly into the kitchen.

"He's gone," she said when he stopped in the doorway, looking rested, but wearing jeans and a polo shirt. He'd find out soon enough what summer in Davis was. She hoped he owned shorts. She'd bet he had great legs. And shoulders, and—

"I heard him go out the back door not too long ago," he said. He came into the room. "Good morning."

"The same to you. Breakfast is ready."

"I see that. Thank you. It's a nice surprise." He took a seat. "Did you sleep all right?"

"Dead to the world. How about you?"

"Half dead." He smiled. "Kind of a lot on my mind."

She put their plates on the table, feeling his gaze on her. She was used to men taking second looks at her, especially at her weekend job, wearing what she wore. Eric took one look...that lasted a long time. And unlike with most other men, she was not only flattered but wishing she could take a good long look at him in return.

"Coffee?" she asked, distracting herself.

A couple of seconds passed before he answered. "Yes, please. Black." He stared at something on the counter, leaned back and grabbed the plastic container with the chocolate-chip cookies. He shook it. Empty. "He feels no qualms about eating and running, obviously."

She shuddered. "It's just creepy knowing that someone can come and go while you sleep and never know it."

"Survival instincts. He's probably gotten good at not making noise."

"Are you going to file a police report?"

"No."

"Good." She sipped from her mug, studying him over the rim. Easy on the eyes, she thought again. She opened a notebook she'd brought downstairs with her. "Here's a list of all the work that's been done, what I think needs to be done, and the contacts I've gathered.

The receipts are in an envelope taped to the inside back cover."

"You've been very efficient. I very much appreciate all you did. Including fixing breakfast," he added, toasting her with a forkful of omelet.

"If there's anything else you need before I go, just ask." She held her breath, not knowing if she wanted him to ask her to stay or let her go.

"Do you have another job to get to?" he asked, choosing a cluster of grapes.

"I did have, but it got canceled."

He tossed a grape in his mouth and chewed, looking at her thoughtfully. "Do you live in Davis?"

"I live everywhere. Davis, Sacramento, Folsom, Roseville. You name it."

"What does that mean? Are you homeless?" He sat back, looking shocked.

"Technically, but it's entirely my choice," she insisted. "If I don't have a house-sitting job, I bunk with a friend in Sacramento. I always, well, almost always have a place to stay."

"Is that where you'll go today?"

"No. We thought I'd be house-sitting, so she invited her parents to come for a week."

The doorbell rang before she could add something that didn't make her sound pathetic.

"That's probably the guy to fix the window lock," she said as Eric left the table, taking a piece of toast with him. She grabbed a cluster of grapes and followed, notebook in hand to remind herself of the man's name. It wasn't the handyman, however.

"I locked myself out." Dylan stood on the porch, his

hands shoved in his pockets, shoulders hunched, staring at his feet.

"Make eye contact, Dylan," Eric said. "Talk to me man-to-man."

The teenager fought it for a few seconds, then put his shoulders back and lifted his head. "I didn't want to wake you up, so I went for a bike ride to kill time. I wasn't running away."

"Are you hungry?" Eric asked.

The boy looked startled, then he nodded.

"Even after eating a dozen chocolate-chip cookies?" Eric stepped back so that Dylan could come inside.

"*Three* dozen," Marcy said, torn between hugging the kid and shaking him.

"They were good," Dylan said, offering the barest smile. "Best I've ever had."

She sighed. "Do you like omelets?"

"I'm not picky."

"Go wash up." She headed into the kitchen, ate the last few bites on her plate then went to the stove. She could hear them talking in the living room but, unlike the night before, she only caught words now and then. Soon Eric returned and sat at the table to finish eating.

"You didn't look surprised to see him," Marcy said quietly to him.

"Having taught for a long time has given me insight. But also, starting when I was twenty-two, I raised my four younger siblings. I got pretty good at reading teenagers."

She stared at him, surprised, although after thinking about it, she realized she could see him in that role. Some people were born to be parents, were born protective and paternal.

"Is that what you meant when you said you'd raised one family?"

"Yes."

"You had to know I would think you were at least fifty, if not sixty, years old."

"I was having fun with you."

And she'd started hunting for a woman for him, someone age appropriate, as he'd said. This changed everything—

Well, maybe not. There was still Annie, next door.

"Have you ever been married?" she asked.

"No. Have you?"

"Guess." She smiled.

Dylan came in and took a seat.

"Grab yourself something to drink," Eric said, refilling his coffee mug before Marcy could wait on either of them. Then Eric's phone rang. He looked at the screen, grabbed Marcy's notebook and pen and left the room.

"You can butter the toast when it comes up," Marcy said when Dylan had poured himself a glass of orange juice.

He moved close to the toaster, leaned against the counter and gulped down the entire glass of juice then refilled it.

"Where's your stuff?" she asked.

"Stuff?"

"Change of clothes. Toothbrush. Stuff."

"In my backpack. Out in the yard, with my bike."

"If you'd like to use the washer and dryer, now's the time." She slid the omelet onto his plate as he buttered the toast.

He dug into the food as he had the night before, barely tasting it, just shoveling it in.

She filled her mug and sat across from him.

"I've never seen hair like yours," he said, catching her off guard, his mouth full. "Not red but not brown either."

She ran a hand down it. She'd let it grow to the middle of her back, only occasionally pulling it into a ponytail when it was going to get in her way. "Is that a compliment?"

He shrugged. "It's nice."

"So you weren't raised by wolves."

He laughed, bits of toast flying.

"How did you know when to break in?" *By watching me?* she thought, realizing he had to have done so.

"There's no curtains. You were always working. Cleaning. I only watched the house to see when you turned out the lights, then I waited a while before I came inside."

"Where'd you sleep? There wasn't any furniture until yesterday."

"On the floor in the dining room."

"When would you take off?"

"First light."

"Why'd you take care of the cardboard and the other stuff? Why'd you do dishes?"

"I was paying for my keep where I could. You shouldn't ever hire that drywall guy again, by the way. He should've cleaned up his own mess."

"I'll remember that, thanks. I'm Marcy, by the way."

Eric returned. He set his cell phone and the notebook on the kitchen counter. "Change of plans. I'm starting work on Monday instead of four weeks from now. One of the professors had emergency heart surgery. They need me to fill in for the remainder of the summer session."

"Teaching what?" Marcy asked.

"Vector analysis."

She exchanged a look with Dylan. "Which is what?"

"Simplified, it's multivariable calculus."

"That's simplified, huh?"

He almost smiled. "I could give you a few paragraphs of further definition, but I thought to spare you that."

"Thank you," she said dramatically, making Dylan laugh. She looked at her watch. "I should probably get going. I'll do the dishes first."

"Dylan will do the dishes," Eric said. "He obviously knows how."

"I don't mind—" She stopped at his I'm-in-charge-here expression. "Okay."

Eric eyed them both. "Here's the deal. I'd expected to have a month to work on the house. I wanted to do a lot of the work myself, to have that personal satisfaction. Now I'll be gone three-to-four hours a day, Monday through Thursday, plus prep work, plus I have my fall classes to prepare for."

"Guess you couldn't turn down the job, huh?" Marcy asked.

"I could have, but it seemed wiser to say yes. Goodwill adds up, especially when you're the new guy."

"I understand that," she said. "Sometimes we have to do what we have to do."

Eric studied her, trying to keep his eyes on her face. Ever since he'd walked into the kitchen earlier and had seen her standing there wearing shorts and a tank top he'd been forcing his gaze above her shoulders, with only occasional success. He'd always been drawn to slender, athletic, quiet women. Marcy laughed easily and with open pleasure. She wore her hair down, untamed, and was all tempting curves. He wouldn't mind running his hands—

Someone kicked him under the table, yanking him out of his fantasy.

"Dude," Dylan said, looking embarrassed.

Had Marcy caught him staring, too? "Sorry. Too much on my mind. I lost my train of thought."

"You were about to offer me a job," Dylan said, angling toward him as if persuading him with body language alone.

"What makes you think that?"

"Your hands are soft. Do you know anything about remodeling or yard work?"

Marcy leaned both elbows on the table and pressed her mouth against her fists, her eyes sparkling.

Eric looked at Dylan again. "Do *you*?"

"More'n you, I bet."

Eric wondered what had brought the kid out of his shell. "You might be surprised. I've been living in New York City for the past twelve years, but before that I did plenty of home repair and yard work." Which wasn't entirely true. He'd made his siblings help, too. Building character, he'd always told them. "What experience do *you* have?"

"I've earned my keep here and there. You planning on remodeling in here?"

"I expect to gut the kitchen and all the bathrooms. Kitchen first. Bathrooms as I have time."

"I'm a hard worker." Desperation overrode Dylan's usual attitude. "I don't know much about plumbing or electrical stuff, but I know what tools do what. Maybe I don't look strong, but I am. I can demo the kitchen, haul everything out. I could do that while you're at work, no problem."

How long had the boy been on the streets? Long enough to become a hustler? Would the cops have known that about him?

Marcy didn't interrupt the conversation, but she was obviously interested.

"You said you don't have another job lined up," he said to her. "And nowhere to live."

"Just my regular Saturday job tonight."

"Wait. You're homeless?" Dylan asked.

"Not in the way you are, but technically, yes."

He frowned, as if the concept was beyond his comprehension.

Eric took charge again. "Here's what I'm proposing. Dylan, I could use you to do exactly what you just said—demo the kitchen, but also work in the yard. It would save me from hiring a gardener for the cleanup. Do a good job and you'll have a reference to use when you apply for work elsewhere."

Dylan's mouth tightened. "You ever try to apply for work when you don't have an address?"

"No, I never have. Maybe we can figure out a way to deal with that. Marcy, if you would stay on, too, I could use you to supervise the work people and also pitch in where you can. We'll discuss wages later. Would that be possible?" He wasn't sure how well he was going to deal with having her around all the time when he wanted to sleep with her. But she was a hard worker and a known quantity. He just needed to keep a rein on his hormones, which had sprung to life in a big way since he'd first seen her last night.

"We'll talk," she said.

"If you stay, so can Dylan. Sorry," he said to the boy, "but I don't know you well enough to leave you here alone all day."

Marcy's expression said it all—she knew he was playing on her sympathies for the teenager. "We'll talk," she said again, more coolly.

He respected her for not letting him ramrod her, but he figured she would end up saying yes, anyway. He'd learned a lot about her sense of responsibility during their phone calls as he'd driven across the country, plus he saw she had a soft spot for the boy.

He also figured he would be helping her out, because she didn't have another house-sitting job to go to. Win-win.

Dylan stood. "You go talk. I'll do the dishes."

"Shall we?" Eric asked Marcy. "Upstairs?"

She sighed but she went with him, leading the way up the staircase, her hips in his direct line of sight. He wished they were going up more than one flight.

They went into his bedroom, the only upstairs room containing furniture. He shut the door, then offered her the bed to sit on. She perched on the edge. He went to stand by the window, looking out at the tree-lined street. He hadn't lived in a neighborhood like this since his sister, Becca, had left for college and he'd sold the family house and moved to New York to teach at NYU.

"It's a pretty neighborhood," Marcy said. "I hope you like kids, because the block is full of them. It can get noisy. Although that'll change when school starts again."

"I do like kids. I intend to have a few of my own. How about you?"

Her brows arched, as if questioning his right to ask that—or perhaps at the fact he wanted a few, not a couple, of kids.

"Not anytime soon," she said.

"Why not?" He put up a hand. "Sorry. None of my business."

"It's fine. I'm only twenty-eight, and right now I have goals to meet. Finish college, decide on a career. That's critical to me. And, no, I haven't been married."

He couldn't have said why, but he hadn't pegged her for a career woman. She seemed to be a nurturer, a stay-at-home-mom type. Maybe he'd read too much into their conversations.

"Your neighbors are looking forward to meeting you," she said.

He'd lived in the same co-op for years and had known only one neighbor to speak to. The personable Marcy had already paved the way for him here not just to meet neighbors but make friends.

"What did you tell them about me?" he asked, moving away from the window.

"I had nothing to offer. For all I knew, you were a doddering old man looking for a nubile young wife to give you a second passel of kids to prove to the world you were still virile."

He laughed. "I hope I've got a long way to go before I hit that stage."

She cocked her head. "You should laugh more often. It takes years off you."

So she *did* think he seemed old? Was an eleven-year age difference that big?

"I shared nothing with your new neighbors, not even

your name," she said, getting back to business. "I figured you would tell them what you want to."

"Thank you. So. What do you think about staying on here?"

"I think you shouldn't have asked me in front of Dylan, because if I say no now, he's going to hate me."

Eric continued to admire her refreshing directness. People tended to tiptoe around him, although he had no idea why. He didn't think he was intimidating. "I apologize."

"That didn't sound very sincere."

He liked that she didn't mince words. For some reason, he found it incredibly sexy. "I admit I should have waited, but I was caught off guard by the phone call from the university. I was in solution mode."

"Now *that* I can buy." She gestured for him to sit on the bed. "I don't like having to look up at you."

He did as she asked.

"What do you see as my role?" she asked.

"Obviously Dylan can't work alone here. He's not a professional. What if something happens? Plus we know little about him."

"You need me to supervise?"

"Yes, but not just Dylan. I'll be hiring out some work I would've done myself. I need an adult here to oversee."

She seemed to consider it. "I could do that, I guess. I start my new semester of college on Tuesday, but they're online classes, and I could do that work at night, at whichever friend's house I land in. As long as I have my laptop, I'm good to go."

"Um. I guess I didn't make myself clear. I'd like you to stay here."

"Stay here? You mean *sleep* here? Why?"

It hadn't occurred to him she wouldn't spend the night. "If you're willing, I'd like you to take on the role of cook. I want to work on the house as much as possible and not worry about the day-to-day home details."

"You're not going to have a kitchen, remember? Isn't that your first project? To demo the kitchen?"

Actually, he'd forgotten. "The truth is I want to give the kid a break, all right? This is the best way I can think of to help."

"And you're willing to pay me to stay so that you can do that?"

"You'd be earning your keep." He must be losing his touch. He could usually talk a person into doing something without a whole lot of effort.

"So, what you're looking for is a wife. Someone to watch over the house and the kid."

He'd already told her that was exactly what he was looking for—and not just temporarily. Maybe she hadn't believed him. Maybe she thought he'd been kidding around about that.

"My understanding is that Julia's agency has been nicknamed 'Wives for Hire,'" he said as an answer. "There must be a good reason for that."

After a moment, she eased off the bed and went to stand where he had earlier, looking outside. He waited her out. The more he watched her, the more she appealed to him, especially physically.

"Here's the deal, Eric," she said finally. "You have to promise not to back me into a corner again. If you want something, ask me privately."

"I promise."

There was a knock on the door. "Sorry," Dylan called out. "There's a guy here to fix the window lock."

"I'll be right there," Eric said, standing. He joined Marcy at the window. He was tempted to run his hand down her billowy hair, to see if it was as soft as it looked. He sensed she was as attracted as he was— which could become a complication.

Or perhaps a solution. Wouldn't it be amazing if she turned out to be the one?

"I'm only doing this for Dylan," she said.

Her defensiveness caught him off guard. Was he standing too close? Her breath was shallow and quick, her eyes wide. She crossed her arms, as if that would help. Attracted? Yes. Afraid of it? Maybe so.

"Whatever the reason, I thank you," he said.

They went downstairs together. He was completely aware of her while at the same time conscious of Dylan's hopeful look. Eric almost sighed. He'd thought he was done parenting teenagers. Apparently not.

Marcy took the workman into the dining room, leaving Eric to give Dylan the news. "She's agreed to stay."

Dylan swallowed and nodded.

"You're welcome to live in or come during the day to work, whichever you prefer, but make a choice and stick to it. Prove you're responsible."

Dylan stuck out his hand. "I'll stay. Thanks."

Eric shook his hand, then gripped the boy's shoulder. "Task number one. Go upstairs and take a shower. When you're done, we'll get started."

Dylan flew up the stairs, scooping up a backpack from the first step. Eric was both grateful and disappointed that Dylan had decided to live in, thus preventing Eric from being alone with Marcy. Except if it hadn't been for Dylan, he wouldn't have asked her to stay. Additionally, he didn't have time to spend on a woman who wasn't looking for the same things he was, no matter how attracted to her he was. He wanted a wife, soon. He wanted to start a family soon after.

It would be wrong to act on the attraction, even if mutual, when it couldn't go anywhere.

Now if he could only convince himself of that.

Chapter Four

Marcy was unpacking boxes in the living room when she spotted Shana Callahan's car pull up. The lively, blonde interior designer had arrived yesterday just before the moving van and spent most of the day placing furniture. She was a human dynamo, and had stopped only to eat a sandwich Marcy shoved at her.

Today she hadn't come alone. Her passenger was a slender woman with chin-length, light brown hair. She carried a huge cellophane-wrapped basket, while Shana lugged a tool box. Both women were about the same age as Marcy.

"I recognize that laugh," Eric called out, emerging from the kitchen as the women reached the screen door.

The brown-haired woman shouted his name. He smiled broadly, then his gaze went tender as she set down her gift and hugged him.

Finally she leaned back, her hands resting on his chest. "I was going to surprise you and be here when you arrived. How dare you be ahead of schedule."

"Yes. So unlike me."

She laughed and stepped away, letting Shana hug him hello, too. "Hi, Marcy," Shana said. "Have you recovered from yesterday?"

"I've worked some of the kinks out. How about you?"

"I feel pretty good, thanks."

"Marcy, this is my sister, Becca Callahan," Eric said. "Becca, this is Marcy Monroe. My wife."

Becca's eyes opened wide. "Wife? What? Since when? I can't believe you—"

"My wife for hire," Eric said, interrupting.

After a moment she laughed but gave him a playful shove. "Payback, hm?"

He grinned.

Fascinated by their easy relationship, Marcy found herself envious, too. An only child, she'd never had a sibling to joke around with.

"I got my husband through At Your Service," Becca said. "Rumor has it so have several others."

The conversation was freaking Marcy out—there was no other way to describe it. People actually found spouses by hiring them to *be* spouses? She'd worked there for four years and hadn't heard that. "Are you serious, Becca?"

"On my honor. I hired Gavin as my temporary husband. We got married two months ago. He would've come today, but he had a baby to deliver."

"He's a doctor," Eric said to Marcy. "He's also Shana's brother."

Dylan had come into the room, his hands stuffed in

his pockets. He was wearing a T-shirt and sweatpants of Eric's while his clothes were in the wash, the too-large clothing making him look even skinnier.

"This is Dylan. He's our baby on the doorstep," Eric said with a wink at Marcy.

Becca and Shana stared at Dylan. Marcy was fascinated by Eric's sense of humor, and how he seemed to enjoy shocking his sister.

"They caught me breaking and entering," Dylan said, standing straighter, as if ready to take his punishment.

"Are you under house arrest?" Becca asked.

"More like community service," Eric said, then glanced at Shana. "You come bearing tools."

"Good," Dylan said with obvious relief. "He only has a hammer and one screwdriver. And soft hands."

"I come bearing gifts, too." Becca untied the ribbon on the basket, revealing champagne and a lot of sweet and savory snacks. "I'm ready to work," she said. "But show me around first, please."

"You didn't bring a crowbar, by any chance, did you?" Dylan asked Shana as Eric led his sister on a tour.

"I did. It's in my trunk, along with more tools, power and otherwise. There are some boxes of light fixtures in the backseat." She tossed him her keys. "If you wouldn't mind."

"Nope." He took off.

"Well," Shana said, looking bewildered.

Marcy laughed. "Didn't expect to find me here, I'll bet."

"Nor the teenager. What happened?"

Marcy gave her a rundown of the previous night's events. "And if I'm right in thinking that Eric had planned to learn as he went in remodeling the kitchen and bathrooms, he needs more help than just Dylan's."

"I know someone who would make himself available, so don't worry about it. Just let me know if you think Eric is in over his head." She looked around. "Are you working from a list?"

"I'm just emptying boxes. Tell me what you need me to do."

They all got busy. Neighbors dropped by with cookies and other welcome gifts. One explained about the Neighborhood Watch program, although he didn't admit to having called the police about Dylan. He supplied Eric with a list of his neighbors and their addresses and phone numbers, as well as the news that the block had a party every Labor Day, which was only a couple of weeks away.

Curious kids tagged along with their parents, too, some shy and clingy, some bold enough to run through the first story, making the circuit from living room to kitchen to dining room to hall and back.

Marcy kept her eye out for his neighbor Annie, but she never showed. Obviously Eric wasn't going to be a fit for Marcy, since they had entirely different goals. Annie could be the one, however. Marcy needed to arrange a meeting.

For lunch, Eric ordered in pizza. By the time Marcy had to get ready for work, all of the window coverings and light fixtures were installed, artwork had found homes and clothing was put away. Going through his possessions had given Marcy a better picture of who Eric was. Even his casual clothes were pressed, including his jeans. He owned many suits—and also a tux. All of his dress shirts were white and his ties plain, muted colors. His dress shoes were polished, his athletic shoes in good condition. Every sock had a mate.

He wore briefs. Ordinary white briefs that seemed incredibly sexy to her.

"Get a grip," she muttered to herself as she shut his dresser drawer then sat cross-legged on the floor, thinking. For the first time, she wanted to call in sick to work. She'd had so much fun with everyone. Shana made list after list of things to buy and people to call. She'd stopped Eric and Dylan from tearing down the kitchen until they had a Dumpster in place and new cabinets ready to install—which had made Marcy laugh. She'd assumed he'd ordered them in time to coordinate with his arrival.

The only awkward moment had come when Marcy set a box of framed photos in front of him and asked which ones he would like displayed. He'd taken out a few then returned them right away and closed the lid, saying he'd figure it out later.

His expression had changed, too. He'd clearly been enjoying himself all day, but seeing the photographs had poked a hole in his playfulness, deflating the mood, and then never quite recapturing it.

"Are you okay?" Eric asked from beside her.

Marcy jolted. He'd come into his bedroom and crouched next to her without her hearing him. She wanted to put her hands against his face in comfort for whatever was hurting him.

"I'm great," she said. "I've had fun today. I like your sister a whole lot."

"Me, too." He smiled. "She turned out okay, despite my overprotectiveness and high expectations. I'd say she survived having four big brothers pretty well."

"She told me the story about how she met her husband."

He nodded. "I can laugh about it now. It was hard to swallow then."

"Do you believe in love at first sight, like she does?" Marcy held her breath. She had no right to ask him such a question. He was her employer, even if only temporarily, and she found him incredibly, inappropriately sexy and appealing, but she really shouldn't be so personal.

Still, she couldn't take back the question.

"I don't know," he said, his gaze direct. "I haven't experienced it myself."

Which gave her an answer in itself. He hadn't fallen for anyone at first sight, therefore he hadn't fallen for her. A stifling blanket of disappointment dropped over her.

Which was totally ridiculous, she realized. Why should she be disappointed?

"Now, lust at first sight? That's different." He took a lock of her hair in his hand and rubbed it. "It's soft. I've been wondering."

"You have?"

"Since first sight."

"Which was only—" she did some quick calculations "—seventeen hours ago."

"First sight," he repeated.

She couldn't believe they were having this conversation. Nothing had preceded it—except some hot looks at each other and conversations mostly taking place in front of others.

"Does that worry you?" he asked. "Too much pressure?"

"I don't know what to think. Maybe I can give you

an answer after work—or tomorrow, since I won't be home—" She caught herself. "I mean back here, until long after you're in bed."

"Tomorrow, then." He stood, held out his hand and helped her up.

For a moment she thought he would kiss her, and she wasn't ready for that, no matter how much she wanted him to. She felt a sudden, overwhelming need to be cautious.

"I need to shower and get going," she said.

He blinked—as if he'd been hypnotized and had just come back to awareness. "I'm—Wow. I'm sorry if I crossed a line, Marcy." He plowed his fingers through his hair. "I don't know what got into me."

She was torn between being happy he couldn't help himself and annoyed that he'd apologized for it. "It's fine," she said.

He backed away and then left the room. Twenty minutes later she went downstairs to tell everyone goodbye. Dylan wasn't in sight, but the others were relaxing in the living room as if they were winding down, too. Conversation stopped as soon as they saw her. Had they been talking about her?

"How often *do* you?" Shana asked, her eyes sparkling.

"Do what?"

"Score."

Oh. They'd stopped talking because of her uniform T-shirt with the name of the bar emblazoned across it. "Not nearly enough."

The women laughed. Eric just watched her. Intently.

Her goodbyes made, Marcy rushed off, welcoming the noise and activity at Score. She'd told him she would think about whether she believed in lust at first sight, but maybe she didn't need to, now that she thought he was embarrassed that he'd asked the question.

Or perhaps she shouldn't give it much thought at all. Maybe she should just live and let live, go with the flow—ignore it until it went away.

She would take her cue from him. If he brought it up again, she would figure out her answer. If he didn't, she wouldn't bring it up.

Except now she knew he'd experienced lust at first sight—with *her.* And that could change everything.

Eric hadn't meant to stay up so late. He was bone-tired but wide awake. His move to California was supposed to uncomplicate his life, so why was he so keyed up?

Dumb question.

A better question would be why had he come on to Marcy as he had? He may have experienced lust at first sight before, but he hadn't acted on it so quickly. It was as if he'd had no control over his actions.

Which was nothing at all like him.

Even his sister had picked up on it. "So, are you happy or unhappy that you have a teenage chaperone around?" Then she'd patted his cheek and left.

And now he was sitting in his living room at almost one o'clock in the morning, the television on to…whatever, as he waited for Marcy. He had to know she got home safely.

He heard her car pull into the driveway and turned off the TV. He should've relaxed but became more tense instead. At this time last night he was just meeting her. Now he felt responsible for her.

The front door opened quietly. She tiptoed in, slipping her shoes off before she shut and locked the door behind her, then she jumped when she saw him sitting there, watching.

"How was your night?" he asked.

"Good. Exceptionally good, actually. People were in a tipping mood. Where's Dylan?"

"We bought another cot. He's in the third bedroom. Do you go straight to bed after work, or do you take time to unwind?" He hadn't moved. Couldn't move. The sight of her in her server's outfit, her hair down and toes bare except for bright red polish, froze him in place.

He'd never felt like this before. Not even close.

"I usually need a little down time," she said, taking a seat in a matching chair across from him. "Why aren't you in bed?"

Tell the truth or lie? Maybe something in between. "I didn't feel ready to sleep."

She didn't question his reason. Was it because she didn't want to answer the query he'd posed before she'd left for work? "I took Dylan shopping for clothes tonight, too. His were in bad shape."

"Softy." She smiled. "Did you find out anything about him? Why he's been living on the streets?"

"He let it slip that his father was a carpenter."

"One discovery at a time, I guess." She crossed her legs. Her foot bounced. When the conversation didn't pick up again, she headed for the stairs. Once there, she hesitated then came back to where he sat. "I don't believe in love at first sight, either, Eric. But lust is a different matter."

Because he was tempted to pull her onto his lap, he stood, his gaze never leaving hers. "What should we do about it?" he asked but didn't wait for her answer. He framed her face with his hands, moved closer and then he kissed her. He wanted to keep it short and tender—best intentions and all that—but the reality was that he couldn't. She tasted of summer, like a vacation in paradise, where every desire was met.

He took it deeper, ran his hands down her back, over her perfect rear, felt her breasts pressing against his chest.

Pulling back, she leaned her forehead against his shoulder, her breath shaky. "That's a good start, I think," she said, then she ran her hands down his chest and went up the stairs.

In a minute he would follow, but to his own room, alone and unsatisfied, but expectation simmering in a way he appreciated, energizing him. He had a new house and a new job in a new city and state. His sister lived an hour away. And he'd already fallen in lust, even if he didn't know what to do about it yet.

All in all, it was a very good start indeed.

Chapter Five

"I'm just a glorified babysitter," Marcy said to her best friend on the phone. It was Monday morning and Eric was off to his first day of teaching, leaving behind a short list of jobs. "There's little for me to do except watch over Dylan while he works in the yard. I'm not even allowed to help because Eric wants there to be enough work for Dylan to last a while."

"Let me see if I've got this straight," Lori Jorgenson said in a musing tone. "You're getting paid for basically sitting around and doing nothing, with full room and board thrown in...and you're complaining? Hold on a sec, Marcy. *Boys!* Stop that right now or you're in time-out!" A pause ensued, then she said, "It sounds like a vacation to me. I haven't had one of those in four years."

Marcy had been standing at the kitchen window

keeping an eye on Dylan as he mowed the lawn—or, more properly, weeds, before moving on to trimming old rosebushes. She turned away from the window. "You're right. I'm being childish."

"Agreed. So what's really going on with you?"

Marcy and Lori had been best friends since the third grade. They'd shared the good, the bad and the ugly. For the moment Lori was dependent on Marcy, but that would change soon. "He—Eric—is very attractive."

"Okay. So?"

"So, it's driving me crazy. He looks at me like no one else ever has."

"Even your customers at Score?"

"It's different. The guys at Score flirt, but I think it's because it's expected of them or something, especially when there's a group of them. For the most part it's a game. They know it, and I know it. With Eric, it's… more intense. More personal. I think if Dylan hadn't been here, we might have already slept together."

"After knowing him for two days? Marcy, that's nothing like you."

Lori was right. She'd made a pact with herself when she was a flight attendant years ago that she wouldn't sleep with a man until she knew him well. Sometimes it had been hard, but she'd kept that promise to herself. She rubbed her forehead now, more confused than ever. "I know. I'm having a hard time fighting my feelings this time."

"How old is he?"

"Thirty-nine."

"And he's never been married?"

"No."

"Then he knows exactly what he's doing. He's a

seducer, Marcy. You need to get out of there ASAP.
Don't you know professors are notorious love-'em-and-
leave-'em guys?"

Because Lori's ex-husband had walked out four years
ago, leaving her with two young sons and no career with
which to support them, she thought no man could be
trusted. "He seems very responsible," Marcy said hesitantly, not wanting to get into a debate. "He raised his
four siblings after their parents died."

"Well, I don't know about that, but I do know you
promised me you wouldn't get married before you finished college and had a career to support yourself. You
don't want to end up like me, do you? Or plenty of other
women in the same boat."

"Who's talking marriage?" A bit of panic set in at
the idea. "I said we were attracted to each other."

"It's more than that. You're hot for each other. That's
stronger and much more dangerous. That's when you
leap without first looking to see how steep the fall is."

Marcy hated to admit it, but she kind of liked the
idea of that. She was rarely impulsive, at least about
matters of the heart. And every time she looked at Eric,
her heart pounded like a big bass drum—not to mention the rest of her body. She caught him watching her
in return, knew he went out of his way to touch her—
setting his hands on her waist as he moved past her, or
a quick shoulder rub when she tried to ease the kinks
out on her own.

She hadn't shied away from his touch, nor had he
from hers. She'd done the same, touching him when
opportunities arose. They'd about reached fever pitch,
and she still had five days remaining before she had to
leave to start a new house-sitting job.

"Are you there?" Lori said in her ear.

"You've given me things to think about."

"Good. You know I want you to be happy, but a man like Eric? There's no future there."

"I know you're right." *But it feels so good....*

A shout came from the backyard. Marcy turned and saw Dylan grip his arm, blood pouring between his fingers. "I have to go," she said to Lori, then grabbed some paper towels and raced outside.

"What happened?" she asked as she ran toward him.

"I had the damn clippers in my pocket and I fell on them." He swore a blue streak.

"Let me see," she said when she reached him, her stomach clenching. *It's just blood. You can do this. You can do this.*

He lowered his arm. Blood flowed anew. She tried to staunch it with the paper towels. He shouted in pain.

"Need some help?" called a woman whose head appeared above the fence. It was Annie. "I'm a nurse."

"Yes!" Marcy and Dylan yelled at the same time.

It seemed like an hour passed before Annie came through the gate and into the yard, carrying a first-aid kit.

"Sit down," she said as she dropped to her knees and opened her kit. "I'm Annie. What's your name?"

"Dylan." He grimaced when she peeled back the towels.

"How old are you?"

"Eighteen. Ow! That hurts," he said as she pressed the towels against the wound again.

"Sorry. Can't help it." She continued to hold it tight, then looked at Marcy. "You said you're not the owner?"

"That's right. I'm just helping him out. Is Dylan going to be okay?"

"I can't see the damage until the blood flow slows. I'm sure he'll live." She smiled at Dylan. "When was your last tetanus shot?"

"Don't know."

"Then you'll need one. What kind of insurance does your father have, do you know?"

"He's not my father. I'm helping, like Marcy. I don't have insurance."

She took a look at the wound. "Needs some stitches," she said. "There's an urgent-care clinic a couple of blocks from here. Keep the pressure on it until you get there." She patted his shoulder. "You'll be fine. You may have to lay off any heavy lifting for a few days, but you won't have permanent damage."

Marcy ran into the house to get clean towels, her purse and car keys then met Dylan and Annie out front. Armed with directions, Marcy took off. At the first intersection she looked at Dylan and saw his eyes tearing up.

"She said you would be okay," Marcy said softly.

"You think I care about that?" he asked, his voice harsh and pain-filled. "I don't give a crap about it. But now I'll be useless to Eric. How can I stay if I can't help?" A tear rolled down his cheek.

"He won't make you leave," Marcy said, sure of it.

"He's always talking about being a man. A man works. A man is responsible. Look at me!" He gestured toward his arm with his chin.

"I think you're underestimating him. Plus, it happened on his property. He's going to feel responsible."

He looked out the passenger window, trying to wipe his cheeks without letting go of his arm.

"What about your family, Dylan? They should know about this."

"I don't have any family."

She turned another corner and hunted for a sign. "Eric said you told him your dad was a carpenter."

"He wasn't my dad. He was just the man who helped raise me. Now he isn't. I don't want to talk about it. I don't have any family. That's that."

Marcy pulled into the parking lot of the clinic. Then two hours, ten stitches and a tetanus shot later they returned to Eric's house. He dropped onto the sofa.

"You can take something for the pain," she said.

"I'm fine," he muttered, leaning back and closing his eyes, ending the conversation.

She wondered when Eric would be home. The class itself should be over about now, but how long he stayed after was anyone's guess.

To pass time she went into the kitchen and put together a green salad, the chopping and dicing soothing to her. Cooking had become a passion early in her life. She'd had a fairly idyllic childhood with an engineer father and stay-at-home mother. As an adult, she used to see her parents on Sundays for dinner, at least until they moved to Arizona last year. They had a good, solid relationship, and she'd always felt loved, although her love life wasn't something she talked about with her mom.

Marcy looked around the corner of the kitchen and saw that Dylan was still asleep. She finished up the salad and had just set the bowl in the refrigerator when she heard Eric's car pull into the driveway. He got out of the car then walked to the backyard. She met him there.

"Hi. How was your first day?" she asked, seeing him frown at how little had gotten done.

"Busy. What happened here?" He gestured toward the yard. "Or didn't happen, I should say."

"First of all, don't panic. Everything's fine. But Dylan had a small accident involving the clippers." She gave him a rundown of the events. "He's asleep. He's also scared to death of your reaction."

Eric looked away, giving her words some thought. He'd been a tough guardian, according to his siblings. He didn't doubt it for a minute. The responsibility he'd felt for raising them right had weighed heavily on him every minute of every day. But he didn't believe they'd feared him. He'd never laid a hand on any of them.

"Why would he be afraid of me?"

"Not of *you*, Eric. The wound was pretty deep, and he won't be allowed to lift anything for a while. He thinks you'll send him on his way."

He closed his eyes for few seconds. "Okay."

They found Dylan sitting up, looking out the front window at some kids playing a game with a big rubber ball. He had to have heard Eric and Marcy come into the living room, but he didn't look toward Eric. His right arm was bandaged below the elbow. He cupped it protectively with his other arm.

Eric generally had no trouble saying what needed to be said, but he wasn't sure what was right in this situation, so he sat on the couch, facing the boy, whose expression was painful to see. Dylan looked...without hope.

"Tough day, huh?" Eric asked.

"Kinda."

"Does it hurt a lot?"

"Not too bad." He looked straight at Eric. He flexed his other arm. "I'll be fine to keep working."

"Not according to the doctor." Eric saw Dylan cringe as if he'd been hit. "But don't worry. I promised you a job, and when the doctor says it's okay, you'll do that job. For now, your job is to heal."

"I'm telling you, man, I can still work. I can do plenty one-handed."

"We'll take it day by day." He put a hand on Dylan's shoulder. He recoiled enough that Eric let go. "Look. Accidents happen. And this one happened on my property. I promise I won't baby you, although I can't promise the same from Marcy." He leaned toward the boy. "She's already hovering, as you can see."

"No hovering," Dylan said to Marcy.

"No promises," she fired back.

After a few seconds, Dylan shrugged.

Crisis averted. Eric understood pride—he had plenty of it himself—but foolish pride was another thing altogether.

"Are you hungry?" Marcy asked. "Do you want some ibuprofen?"

"I'm okay."

"Don't be a hero," Eric said. "People heal better if they're not fighting pain at the same time."

"Geez. Okay. And yes, I'm hungry."

"Do you play chess?" Eric asked, standing.

"Nope."

"Want to learn?"

"On the computer?"

"No, the real deal, with a board and game pieces."

"I suppose. Hey, look. Out the window. That's Annie. She's the nurse from next door who helped me."

Annie headed up Eric's walkway carrying a foil-covered plate. He guessed her to be in her early thirties. And when he opened the door, he checked to see if she wore a wedding ring, a habit he'd gotten into recently, since he'd embarked on his journey to the next step in his life.

"Hi. I'm Annie Berg." She held a baby monitor and used it to point to the right. "I live next door."

"You're Dylan's angel. I'm Eric Sheridan. Please come in."

She passed him the plate. "These are a combination welcome-to-the-neighborhood and get-well-soon-Dylan gift."

"Thank you. He's right over there." He lifted the foil. Brownies. He tried not to laugh. Her gift made the third batch of welcome brownies from neighbors. "Want a brownie, Dylan?"

"Awesome. Hi, Annie. You were right. Ten stitches."

Eric went into the kitchen, where Marcy was putting a sandwich on a plate.

"Brownies," he said, holding up the dish.

She smiled. "Seems like kind of a down-to-earth gift for an angel of mercy. I have to say, I was really happy when she appeared at the fence. I mean, I would've handled it, but I get a little shaky around blood. Annie was cool and calm. You would've been impressed."

He stroked his chin as if it were a beard. "So, tell me, Ms. Monroe. Were you traumatized in your youth?" he asked.

She grabbed a brownie to add to Dylan's plate. "Prob-ably a repressed memory of having encountered a vampire or something." She poured a glass of milk. "You handled Dylan well. I get the feeling you've done a bit of parenting in your day."

She smiled at him, and then they went into the living room together. Marcy was intrigued by how animated Dylan looked talking to Annie.

"Annie's the one who called the cops on me," Dylan said as Marcy handed him his plate of food. Surprisingly, he was grinning about it. "She says people look out for each other here. That's good, huh?"

He took a bite out of the brownie instead of the sandwich.

"Dylan tells me you're a professor at Davis," she said to Eric, giving him a steady look.

"Right. Math and computer sciences."

"I was a pediatric nurse in the med center there until I had Lucy two years ago. My husband died when she turned one."

"I'm sorry," Eric and Marcy said at the same time.

"Thank you. I have to say, it's great having someone in the house again. It's just you, Eric?" she asked.

Marcy smiled. Annie already knew it was *just him.* Plus she'd changed clothes since she'd helped Dylan earlier and now wore a much lower tank top and shorter shorts. She had the body to pull it off. She was all long legs and perky breasts. And she knew how to fling her hair back in a really sexy way, too.

"Yes, it's just me," Eric answered. "With a little help from my friends. For now, anyway."

He was responding to Annie's flirtation! Maybe he wasn't looking at the woman in the same way he looked at Marcy, but he seemed interested. Then when Annie said she had to go, Eric followed her onto the porch, pulling the door shut behind them then lingering for a while, talking and laughing. Or at least *she* was laughing, as if he was the funniest man on earth.

Which Marcy knew he wasn't. Maybe she needed to rethink trying to get them together.

"Have you got a fire extinguisher?" Dylan asked.

"In the kitchen. Why?"

"'Cause the heat-seeking missiles you're sending Annie's way are gonna light her up like a torch."

Marcy didn't say anything as he climbed off the couch. He patted her on the shoulder and smiled knowingly. She stuck her tongue out, and he laughed. Then he headed on down the hall to the bathroom just as Eric came inside.

"Nice lady," he said. "I sure got lucky with the neighbors I've ended up with."

Marcy counted to five before she responded, "She's fortunate she has a good career to support her and her little girl."

"She's a stay-at-home mom, and intends to be, at least until her daughter starts school. It seems really important to her. Says her career will be there when she's ready. Nursing's a good occupation for the mommy track, she said."

Reluctantly, Marcy admired her again. "It's good she can afford to do that."

"I gather it's not easy, but she's determined."

Dylan joined them.

"It's probably not a good idea to tell everyone you were breaking and entering," Eric said. "People might shy away from you. Or think you're to blame for anything else that might happen."

"*And* question your own competency for keeping him here," Marcy said to Eric, still annoyed at him.

"That, too," he said mildly, but raising his brows slightly.

"I won't tell anyone else," Dylan said. "But was I supposed to lie when she said she'd called the police about an intruder the other night?"

Marcy looked at Eric for an answer but he didn't give one.

"I'll get the chess set," he said instead, and then went up the stairs.

The chess lessons lasted until Dylan dropped off to sleep again. In the kitchen, Marcy had made a marinade for some chicken to barbecue later, then she looked around for something else to do. She went in search of Eric, finding him on the back porch. It was a hundred-and-two degrees, so he was sitting in the shade in a dining-room chair.

"It'll be nice to have backyard furniture," she said, coming up beside him. "Probably by the end of the week, Shana said."

He started to rise.

"Stay put. I'm fine." She leaned against the railing, soaking up a little sun. Having grown up in the Central Valley she was used to the heat. "I need something to occupy my time, Eric. I'm used to working. I like working. Maybe now that things have settled down a little, you could go through your photos and choose the ones you'd like displayed. I could hang them. Lots of people put their family photos up on the wall along their stair-case."

"No. I'll put some in my bedroom, and maybe a

couple on the fireplace mantel, but that's all." His eyes going dull, he looked away.

"Why do those pictures make you sad, Eric?"

"I've been thinking about Annie."

Marcy tried not to overreact to the change in subject. "Oh?"

"Being a single parent is hard."

"She's young." *And beautiful.* "She'll likely remarry."

"And in the meantime, she'll be Mom and Dad. In charge. Responsible for everything herself. No breaks."

Marcy didn't know where he was going with the conversation, what point he was making, so she said nothing beyond a sound of agreement.

"Come with me, please," he said.

She followed him upstairs. Picking up a box from the floor, he set it on his bed. He thumbed through the frames and pulled one out, tenderly brushing his hand across the glass before holding it out to her.

"This is Jamie."

Chapter Six

The picture was his favorite of him and Jamie, taken after a snowstorm in Central Park last January. "He had just turned ten. I'd been his Big Brother for three years. The official rules state that Big Brothers see their Little Brother for at least four hours, twice a month, as well as have regular phone contact. We easily exceeded that every month."

He reached for the picture. Marcy gave it back to him, as well as a large dose of sympathy. "Like Annie, Jamie's mother was a single mom. His dad was never in the picture. When Jamie was nine she met someone and got married. Jamie wasn't bonding with his new stepdad, so I was asked to end our relationship."

Marcy rubbed his back. "I'm sorry. That obviously hurt you."

Hurt? It was such a small word. "Honestly, it broke my heart. And Jamie's."

"It was selfish of his mother and stepdad."

He moved away a little, just far enough that she couldn't touch him. Her sympathy made it worse.

"No, I get it," he said. "I do. After the wedding, Jamie continued to call me with his problems or even just to share his day, as he'd done for years. He needed to let his stepfather into his life, and he wouldn't, not as long as I was there for him to turn to. We'd been Big Brother and Little Brother for three years. That's a lifetime at his age."

"Is that why you left New York?"

"It was a big part of it. But the planets seemed to align, and I knew it was time to make a big change."

"And then the first thing that happens is you kind of end up with a little brother."

He frowned. "Dylan's an adult."

"Who's already dependent on you."

He was aware of that growing dependency. "I can't take him in full-time. I will certainly help him find a path for himself, but I can't be his big brother—or father replacement."

"How about being his friend?"

"I won't throw him to the wolves, Marcy. I just can't offer him a home here."

"Well, since I don't have a place to house him, I can't, either." She crossed her arms. "But I would if I could."

"He's knotted up with anger, can't you tell? Right now we're in the honeymoon phase where his goal is to please. That will change at some point."

"How do you know?"

"Experience. Observation. Study. We don't even

know what he wants. College? A job in a particular field?" His cell phone rang. He saw it was a local number but didn't recognize it.

"Hi, Eric, it's Annie."

"Hello, Annie." He caught a glimpse of Marcy rolling her eyes before she turned around and walked out of the room. What was that about?

"I know this is last minute, but a few of us on the block decided to throw together an impromptu barbecue. Nothing fancy. Just turkey burgers and pasta salad at my place. Would you like to come?"

"I need to check with Marcy. Maybe what she's planned for dinner can keep until tomorrow."

"Um, I don't mean to sound ungracious, but we were really only inviting you, as our new neighbor. Dylan probably shouldn't go anywhere tonight, and I imagine Marcy wouldn't want to leave him alone."

Eric's first inclination was to say no. It had been a long day, his first at a new job, one he hadn't planned on. But he needed to keep a little distance between Dylan and himself. As for Marcy? It was a good idea to keep his distance there, as well. The less temptation, the better.

"Eric? Are you there?"

"When would you like me to come? And what can I bring?"

"Six o'clock. Just bring yourself. It's our welcome to you. I'm so glad you said yes."

They ended the call, then Eric tapped his phone to his chin. Annie was exactly the kind of woman he'd hoped to find. Easy on the eyes. Mature. Cool in a crisis. Competent. She had a two-year-old, so she was already settled. She'd made the decision to put her career on hold for her daughter, which was another pro.

He wasn't attracted to her physically in the same way he was to Marcy. He could hardly take his eyes off Marcy, and spent a lot of time wondering what she looked like without the barrier of clothes. He had a pretty good idea, since he mostly saw her in shorts and tank tops. He and Marcy both touched each other now and then, grazes at first, then longer contact. And then this morning he'd seen her rub her lower back.

"Sore?" he'd asked.

"I'll be okay." She'd busied herself slicing a melon.

He'd debated asking for permission but figured she'd say no, even if she wanted to say yes. So he just went up behind her and massaged her back from shoulders to tailbone. She'd made soft sounds of appreciation that sounded dangerously close to moans. He'd just pressed his lips to the tempting spot below her ear when Dylan came flying down the staircase, sounding more like a herd.

Eric had stepped away. If they'd only had a few more minutes... .

He shook off the image and went downstairs, finding Marcy in the kitchen, sliding a baking dish into the oven.

"I've been invited to meet some of the neighbors at Annie's for dinner tonight," he said, feeling like a jerk for not even asking if that interfered with her plans.

"That's great. Have fun."

"I'll be in the dining room working at my computer until then."

"Okay."

He hesitated for a few seconds then started to leave.

"On second thought," she said. "I think I'll go visit a friend. There's really nothing for me to do here. Salad is in the refrigerator. I just put the chicken in the oven. If you'll take it out when the timer rings, Dylan can eat when he's ready. See you sometime tonight. Or tomorrow morning."

She didn't look at him. Not once. Twenty minutes later he heard her come down the stairs. He got to the dining-room door in time to see her leave the house, wearing something that showed off her voluptuous body. He thought maybe it was called a sundress.

He called it sexy, and it made him wonder if this "friend" was male or female.

"I'm sorry I was right about your professor," Lori said as she and Marcy sat on benches, watching Lori's six-year-old and eight-year-old sons play in the park near their apartment. With her petite frame and pixie haircut, Lori hardly looked older than her boys.

"Obviously he's not *my* professor." Marcy was still a little stunned. "I've never seen anyone work so fast. Annie was inside the house for ten minutes and on the porch with Eric for another ten, and he already knew her life story. And he's really protective. It's a big part of who he is. She had him at 'I'm a widow with a baby.' Double whammy for Mr. Protector."

"Wow, are you ever worked up! But Marcy, I don't think you can equate his accepting an invitation to a barbecue to his getting married next week. Besides, isn't that what you'd decided to do? Help him hook up?"

"Not hook up! He's looking to get married, and that's different."

Lori laughed. "I wish I'd recorded this conversation

so I could replay it for you in a month. And I wish I could take pictures of the way *you* look at him. I'll bet they're similar to Annie's expressions."

"Nope. Hers are calculated. Mine are lustful." She grinned, relaxing. Talking with Lori always helped Marcy gain perspective. Today was no different.

"So have a fling with him and be done with it. Hook up."

Is that what she needed? Permission to sleep with the man for no reason other than the desire to? Could she throw caution to the wind? Shouldn't she at least fancy herself in love first?

"You're overthinking it," Lori said, elbowing her. "That's so you."

"I can't believe you're advising me to just go ahead and sleep with him."

"If you'd come to me and said you were in love and wanted to marry the man—after knowing him for only three days—I would be advising you to run. You know that. This is different. If you don't give in to it, you'll obsess. You know what they say about only regretting the things you didn't do."

"Would you do it? Have a fling?"

"If I had the time and energy for one."

"Auntie Marcy! Come push me," the six-year-old shouted as he pulled himself up onto a swing.

"Me, too!" yelled his brother.

Marcy and Lori pushed the boys for a long time. They grabbed a pizza on the way back to Lori's Sacramento apartment, then Marcy hung around until almost eleven-thirty. It was midnight when she pulled into Eric's driveway. The living-room lights were on, otherwise the house was dark. She'd learned he was a night owl, however, a holdover from living in New York, he'd told her.

He was watching television, an old black-and-white Western. He pressed the pause button as she locked the door.

"Did you have fun?" he asked.

"I did. How about you?"

"It was interesting. Dylan went to bed not too long ago."

He really was a strikingly handsome man, Marcy thought. And, in truth, his protectiveness was an appealing trait. So were his arms and chest, and every other part of him….

She sat in the chair across from him, something they'd done every night, almost like a husband and wife catching up or parents finding a little quiet time.

"What other neighbors did you meet?" she asked.

"The couple on the other side of Annie, who are both UC Davis employees, although not teachers. And a couple from across the street, both of them lawyers."

"A street full of professionals."

"Mostly, it sounds like. Annie said there are about thirty kids in a two-block area. We ate turkey burgers."

"Of course you did." Marcy couldn't help but smile. "Organic, I assume."

He smiled, as well. "I didn't ask. What'd you do for dinner?"

"Had pizza. My friend has a couple of boys and they can't afford to go out much. It's a treat. Lori's the one who gives me a place to stay between jobs."

He seemed to relax more. "I waited up to ask you a question."

"Fire away."

"Would you really take Dylan into your home if you had one?" he asked.

"Of course."

"Why?"

"Because he's homeless, and I'm gathering it wasn't a situation he chose. He seems like a good kid."

Eric leaned forward. His voice went quieter. "We don't know anything about him except what he's told us and what little the cops added. He could be on the run from something. We don't even know if Anthony is his real last name. Maybe it's his middle name."

"I consider myself a pretty good judge of character."

"And he could be a pretty good con man. All I'm saying is, be careful. Don't have blind faith. He has two strikes against him, remember?"

"Minor offenses. Stolen cookies."

"Breaking and entering."

"Just because you're cynical doesn't mean I have to be. I've known you the same amount of time as I've known Dylan, and I trust you. Should I not?"

His smile was lopsided. "One of the things I like about you is your directness."

And my body, she thought. But she'd already figured out what he was looking for in a woman—someone educated, someone suitable for this neighborhood. Someone who wanted babies right away. She didn't fit any of the criteria.

"*One* of the things?" she repeated.

"Fishing for compliments?"

"You said *one.* I'm curious to know the others."

He steepled his fingers in front of his face. "You work hard. You don't need to be supervised."

She huffed out a breath. "High praise, indeed. So, do I get a raise, boss?"

He laughed. "Okay, okay. You're enthusiastic and caring and nurturing. Is that better?"

"Much. Would you like to know what I like about you?"

He seemed to consider it. "Narrow it down to one. I like the number one."

"Yes, it comes in handy when working with the binary, doesn't it?" she asked.

"It certainly does."

"One, hm?" She considered and discarded many descriptors.

"Can't do it?" he asked after a while.

"There are a lot of things, but if I have to choose just one, I'll say your sex appeal."

He looked more than a little taken aback, but Marcy didn't know whether it was because she'd chosen that particular feature or the fact she admitted it.

"I would've said that myself about you—the thought did cross my mind—but I'm sensitive to being charged with harassment," he said.

If not for the twinkle in his eyes, she might have taken him seriously. "Will you complain to Julia about me?"

"I'll call her office first thing in the morning." He turned serious then. "Do you run into that problem a lot in your various jobs?"

"Finding my boss sexy?" she asked.

"No. Being harassed by men. Because of the way you look."

This was getting interesting, she thought. "How do I look?"

"Still fishing for compliments?"

"Of course I am. Feel free to be specific." It was an entirely new type of foreplay for her, words instead of touch. She found she liked it—a whole lot.

"I never gave a woman's hair a lot of thought before," he said, studying her. "Subconsciously, I suppose, I did and either liked it or not. But yours makes me want to touch it. To feel it against—" He stopped, as if unsure whether he should continue.

"Don't stop now," she said, her body heating up, tingling with need.

"To feel it against my skin." His voice had gone low and deep. His eyes seemed almost black. "Your breasts are incredible. And you've got a rear made for grabbing." He drew a shaky breath. "Enough specificity for you?"

If anyone had told her that words alone could get her this aroused, she would've laughed. "It's like phone sex without the phone," she said, not knowing what else to say. She couldn't instigate anything physical, no matter what Lori said. Plus Dylan was in the house. "Who would've thought a mathematician could be so hot. Although I guess Annie agrees with me."

"What?" He sat up straight. "What do you mean?"

"Your sex appeal. It's universal, I think." She'd done it now. She'd totally destroyed the mood. Why had she?

Fear. The word bounced around her mind. She was afraid she was falling for him beyond just the physical.

"I've known Annie all of a few hours. She's been neighborly." He sounded annoyed.

Marcy was annoyed at herself for ruining the mood, but especially for putting the idea in his head that Annie was interested when he apparently hadn't seen it for himself. And once someone knows another person is interested, it changes things. He would look at Annie differently now.

The silence between them grew awkward, so she stood and said good-night. As she walked past his chair he wrapped his hand around her wrist, stopping her. He ran his thumb over her skin, barely brushing, thoroughly arousing.

"Maybe you need to have Julia hire someone else for the duration," she said quietly, looking down at him.

"I don't want someone else."

She didn't know how to take that. He didn't want someone else professionally—or personally? "I gather from all you've told me, Eric, you're in mourning for the loss of an important relationship, and your life is a little chaotic, too, with so many changes coming at once. You're in a vulnerable position."

Not releasing her, he stood. He laid his free hand along her face. "I can't deny that, but it doesn't mean I don't know what I want."

For the short term or long? She wondered which as he bent toward her, asking permission with his eyes.

She went up on tiptoe, meeting him halfway. His lips grazed hers, then settled, his tongue finding warm, wet passage, deepening, intensifying. He let go of her hand. She wrapped her arms around him, savoring him, cherishing him, knowing full well it was no way to handle this situation, but unwilling to stop, even if this was the only memory she would have of him.

His arms tightened around her so that there was no space between their bodies, just heat against heat. He changed the angle of his head, attacked her mouth, made throaty sounds of desire. He moved his hands alongside her waist, his thumbs resting under her breasts, pressing, then gliding, moving up a little at a time. He found her nipples, made her ache with need. She wanted his hands on her flesh, not just to feel them through her clothing. She gave him access by tipping her head back when he traced her neckline with his tongue, dipping between her breasts, his breath hot and exciting, his fingers moving along the buttons down her bodice.

Eric straightened, his gaze connecting with hers then lowering as he eased his hands inside her strapless bra, the backs of his fingers gliding over her nipples. If they were alone in house, what would happen next?

He finished unbuttoning her dress and then slipped his hands around her to unhook her bra. "Okay?" he whispered.

"I don't know."

He stopped, torn between wishing he hadn't asked, and amazement that he had the presence of mind not to go forward without her agreement.

"I'm sorry," she said. "I don't mean to tease, but—"

"Don't be sorry. I rushed you. My apologies." He took a step back, giving her room to button up again. "Are we okay?"

"Of course." Her eyes weren't telling him the same thing. She was wary, and maybe scared, but unless he asked why, she probably wouldn't tell him. He didn't want to open a discussion to which he might not like the answers. He'd just never felt like this before, not this fast. Not this intensely.

"I'm going to bed," she said, then rested her hand on his chest for a few seconds.

"Sleep well." He sure as hell didn't think *he* would, however.

"You, too."

He waited until he heard her bedroom door shut before he turned off the television and made his way upstairs. Had they just taken one step forward and two steps back—or two steps forward and one back?

The story of his life lately.

From his bed, he picked up Jamie's picture to set aside, waiting for his chest to start hurting. It didn't. Or at least the pain wasn't overwhelming. Sharing Jamie with Marcy had helped.

A few minutes later Eric climbed into bed.

He thought about Marcy's comments regarding Annie, but it was hard to focus on anything other than the moment he'd just shared with her.

Who could sleep after that?

Chapter Seven

"What's going on with you and Eric?" Dylan asked Marcy a couple of days later. They'd taken sandwiches onto the back porch and were sitting on the deck stairs to eat lunch.

"I don't know what you mean," Marcy said. Except she did. She and Eric weren't arguing. They were avoiding each other. They were polite, but that was all. It didn't help that Annie stopped by every day, usually with her daughter, Lucy, who turned on her cherubic toddler charm full force whenever she saw Eric. He gave her piggyback rides and bounced her on his knee, revealing an entirely different side to him.

He would make an extraordinary father.

"You stopped flirting with him," Dylan said.

She almost choked on her sandwich. "That's crazy. He's my employer. I don't flirt with him."

"You did. Then you stopped. So did he."

She frowned. "We don't have as much to discuss as we did last week. We're waiting on furniture to be delivered, and Shana's bringing a contractor today to measure the kitchen, then work will start on that. At the moment, things here are mostly at a standstill. Plus my online classes have started."

"We both know you're only here to be my keeper. You'd like to leave."

Marcy studied him. Even in such a short time, he'd already filled out a little, and was constantly eating, as if he'd been starved. "I enjoy your company, Dylan."

He sort of laughed. "You're as dumb about this as Eric."

"You talked to him about this?"

"This morning, while you were in the shower."

Marcy was torn between wanting to know what he said, and— No, she wasn't torn at all. "What'd he say?"

"He gave me the look. You know the one I'm talking about?"

She did. Her father had perfected the look himself. It must be embedded in the male DNA. "Why did you ask him?"

"What happens between you and Eric affects me. As long as you're getting along, I don't worry about it."

"And you think we're not getting along?"

"I know things changed."

"Well, everything is fine, so don't worry about it." She appreciated not having a choice in where she lived right now, actually. Yes, she'd stayed because of Dylan—he was right about that—but she wasn't ready to leave Eric, either. "I do have a house-sitting job that starts on Friday."

"I know, but that's three days away. By then, maybe he'll trust me." He took a big bite of his sandwich in a way that showed he was nervous about Eric keeping him on.

"If you'd like to gain his trust, you might think about confiding in him."

A flash of anger crossed his face. Marcy recalled Eric's words about not knowing anything about Dylan.

"No. I pushed my reset button," he said finally.

"Meaning what?"

"I decided to forget about the past. I've started over."

"See, now, I have no idea what that means. Did you do something criminal? Did you hurt someone? Because you don't get to ignore things like that just so you can make a fresh start. You have to face the consequences of your actions first. You have to make amends."

He stood, towering over her. "Even adults don't do that, so why should I?"

He disappeared into the house. He could hole up in what was his bedroom, she supposed, but there was nothing but a cot in it and his meager belongings. No television, no computer.

With a sigh, she carried her empty plate into the kitchen. He stood at the sink eating a cookie, two more in his hand. As soon as he saw her he headed for the back door, rushing past her.

"Going for a bike ride," he muttered.

She glanced at his gauze-wrapped arm. "Be careful."

He stopped at the door, looking more than annoyed. "No, I don't think I will be, Marcy. I think I'll be reckless."

"I didn't—"

"Don't mother me." He left. The only thing that kept

him from slamming the door behind him was the fact the wood was a little warped and had to be pulled shut to close it all the way.

She watched him take off up the driveway. Eric had paid him some wages, so he had money to spend, but he probably wouldn't leave the city limits, given his transportation issues. Besides, Davis was one of the most bicycle-friendly cities in the country, ten square miles of bike paths and plenty of bike racks. It made riding appealing and easy.

Marcy washed their lunch dishes, a mindless chore. For all that Dylan had told her not to mother him, she was pretty sure it was something he needed. Maybe he needed fathering even more, but he also needed the gentle balance of a mother.

What happened to your family, Dylan?

Marcy took advantage of the quiet house to study. This semester she was taking psychology and U.S. history. Both involved a lot of reading and focus. She'd gotten her first homework assignment just today, and she wanted to stay on top of everything.

An hour passed, and Dylan hadn't returned. She shut off her computer, as Shana and the contractor were due any minute, and Eric shortly thereafter. She was headed to the living room when her cell phone rang.

"Hi, Marcy. It's Julia Swanson. How's everything going?"

"It's fine, Julia, thanks. It's turned into a longer job than we originally thought."

"Yes, Eric has stayed in touch."

"Well, if you get any day jobs for next week, that'd be great, too."

"Hm. I gathered Eric still wanted you during the days."

What? "Um. He hasn't talked to me about that."

"I'm sure he will. Let me know what you decide, so I know whether to put you in the available pool."

"While I've got you, Julia. Is there any chance you'd have work for an eighteen-year-old young man? He's a hard worker but he hasn't amassed much in the way of experience yet, obviously."

"Is he presentable?"

"He needs a professional haircut, but yes."

"You know I'm always on the lookout for young people to serve appetizers and drinks at parties and events, but eighteen's pretty young. How do you know him?"

Marcy bit her lip for a second. She couldn't exactly tell the truth. "Eric hired him to help out here, too."

"Well, then, if both you and Eric are recommending him, I'll at least give him an interview."

"I'm not sure I'm recommending him yet, but if you could interview him? Give him that experience? I'd appreciate it."

"Of course I can."

As soon as the call ended, a large pick-up truck pulled in front of the house and parked. Shana emerged from the passenger side. From around the truck came a thirtyish man with a distinctively lumberjack look about him, right down to his work boots. His truck was loaded with cartons.

"We come bearing gifts," Shana said. She looked exceptionally pretty, her blond hair shimmering in the sunlight. Even though it was hot, she came dressed for manual labor in jeans and a T-shirt. She pulled on work gloves as she waited for Marcy to join them. "This is

Landon Kincaid. He prefers to be called Kincaid. I talked him into picking up a few things with me on the way. You've got muscle here, right?"

Marcy greeted Kincaid then said, "Dylan's on the injured reserve list, but Eric's due home any minute." She flexed her muscles. "I'm game, though. What all did you bring?"

"A desk, a real kitchen table to replace the card table, a bed for the guest room. The rest of the guest-room and office furniture will be delivered this afternoon, along with the backyard furniture."

"You've been busy twisting arms," Marcy said. "We didn't expect any of that until later in the week."

"*Persuasive* is her dominant trait," Kincaid said, untying the ropes securing his cargo. "*Never take no for an answer* is her motto."

"And *annoy Shana at every opportunity* is yours," Shana said.

Marcy smiled at the byplay. Were they a couple?

"I don't have time for no's," Shana said. "I have a daughter to support without being away from her sixty hours a week."

"You didn't mention a daughter before," Marcy said. "How old is she?"

"Thirteen months."

"A little one. Does she look like you?" They moved to the back of the truck so that Kincaid could pass them some boxes.

"Twins, separated by a generation," Kincaid said. "And already just as stubborn."

"Are you two—" Marcy gestured to both of them in question, asking a silent question.

"Good grief, no. We're just friends," Shana said.

Intrigued, Marcy considered them as they all unloaded the truck. They so studiously avoided each other—just like Eric and herself, she realized—that she decided there *was* something going on, whether they acknowledged it themselves or not.

Eric pulled into the driveway when the heaviest items were all that remained.

"Where's Dylan?" Eric asked after the introductions, passing Marcy his briefcase before he went to help Kincaid at the truck.

"He went for a bike ride." She aimed for a casual tone, but Marcy took note of the dark expression that crossed Eric.

Marcy put together some snacks and iced tea for everyone while Kincaid measured the kitchen and sketched out a design plan. He and Eric talked about wood finishes, appliances, and flooring. Shana got between them to offer input and suggestions.

Annie dropped by, having seen all the activity, and also got into the middle of the planning. The baby monitor was tucked in her back pocket, the sweet sounds of Lucy reaching them.

"She sings herself to sleep," Annie said with a smile.

Marcy felt like a third wheel. Her opinion wasn't being sought, but then, it wasn't her kitchen. If it were, she'd be setting it up a little differently from the plan being drawn.

She decided to retreat to the backyard, where she sat on the deck stairs and leaned against the post.

So, according to Julia, Eric wanted her to work for him during the day next week. Why? To watch over Dylan, as he'd suggested earlier? Once the rest of the furniture was delivered and placed, there wouldn't be much left to do, certainly nothing that Eric and Dylan couldn't handle, with a little guidance from Shana. And apparently Eric had decided to hire Kincaid, the expert, to install the kitchen, with himself and Dylan as his helpers.

There was still a lot of yard work to be done, as well. And eventually the two-and-a-half bathrooms. She wasn't needed for any of that.

She really didn't see any reason to return next week—or anytime thereafter. With or without her, Eric would either allow Dylan to stay or...

Or what? She didn't know.

Dylan rode into the yard, looking as if the ride had done him a lot of good, happiness showing on his face like a dog's when it had its head out a car window during a drive.

"Hiding out?" he asked, leaning his bike against the deck. "I see the commander-in-chief is home."

She smiled at the title. "Enjoying the sun. Got a second?"

Wariness seeped into his expression. "Yeah. Unless Eric needs me."

"He's occupied. I talked to my boss today to see if she might find placement for you. She says to come in. If nothing else, it'll give you interview practice."

He sat next to her. "What boss?"

"I work for a temp agency. Sometimes they hire helpers for parties or corporate events where servers carry trays of appetizers and drinks through crowds."

He frowned. "I probably need ID, huh?"

"Yes. Why don't you have any?"

"Because someone stole my backpack. I had my cash

in a pouch around my neck. Should've kept my driver's license in there, too, I guess. And some other stuff."

"Personal items?"

He looked out at the yard. "Yeah. Things that can't be replaced."

She laid her hand on his shoulder. He didn't shrug it off, but hung his head.

She pulled back when he finally did shift his shoulders. "Why haven't you replaced your driver's license?"

"And have it sent where?"

Marcy gave it some thought, then she pulled out her phone and dialed. "Hey. Remember me telling you about Dylan? I've got a favor to ask." A minute later she hung up. "My best friend, Lori, lives in Sacramento. She says sure, you can use her address, no problem. Anytime you want to go to the DMV, let me know. I'll take you."

"Thanks," he said, low and gruff, then swallowed hard.

"There you are," Eric said from behind them, coming onto the deck. "Shana and Kincaid are heading out to pick up a few more things. Dylan, please come and meet Kincaid. You'll be working with him."

Marcy and Dylan scrambled to stand. Dylan went inside as Eric delayed Marcy with a hand on her arm.

"Everything okay?" he asked.

"Sure. Did you come up with a design you like?"

"I think so. Kincaid will draw up an official plan and bring it by in a few days."

"That's great." She moved past him, not wanting to keep anyone waiting. Annie was still hanging around, which annoyed Marcy. She was coming to the conclusion that Annie wouldn't be the right person for Eric, after all. He didn't need someone so...perfect. He needed someone to shake up his life a little.

An hour later the furniture truck arrived. Dylan leaned close to Marcy. "That Annie's kinda pushy, isn't she," he whispered.

She lifted her chin. "I have no opinion on the matter."

Dylan laughed, the first true, hearty, appreciative laugh since he'd arrived.

As luck would have it, Lucy woke up from her nap as they all went outside to greet the furniture delivery-men, so Annie excused herself. Finally.

The men carried the office furniture upstairs to Dylan's room, then hauled the guest-room furniture—a headboard, armoire and two nightstands—to Marcy's room. A few more pieces were scattered around the house. Suddenly it seemed like a home, a real home.

She caught Eric realizing it, too. After Shana and Kincaid left, Eric stood in his living room looking around, taking it all in. Dylan was in the office hooking up the various pieces of equipment.

"It looks good, doesn't it?" he said to Marcy.

"It does."

"The pieces Shana chose fit well with what I brought and with the style of this house. She's talented."

"She told me this is only her third paying job as a decorator, your sister's condo being her first, and now Becca's new house, apparently. I really envy natural talent like that."

"I hear she does temp jobs for your agency."

"Yes." And meeting Shana only reinforced Marcy's need to finish her education and establish a career.

Shana was yet another single mom struggling to support herself and her daughter.

Eric eyed the staircase, and then took Marcy by the arm toward the front window. "Is there something I should know about Dylan?"

"Like what?"

"I'm asking you that. He seems to have an attitude today that he hasn't had since the first night."

She had no intention of interfering in their relationship. "Maybe the honeymoon you spoke of is over."

His brows drew together, as if considering it. "Guess he and I need to talk."

He gestured toward what she was coming to think of as the "dialogue chairs." They gravitated toward them every night. Some discussions had been easy, some stilted. Some were filled with annoyance, and some distinctly sensual. What would tonight's be?

"Why'd you leave when we were talking about the kitchen plans?" Eric asked.

"There were a lot of people stirring the pot already. Plus, it's not my kitchen."

"But you have ideas about it."

"I—Well, of course I do. That's only natural. In the end, however, it's your decision."

"What would you do differently?"

She wasn't about to pass up an opportunity to express her opinions. "Where you've got upper and lower cabinets next to the range, I'd put a full pantry. The counter space there isn't very usable, anyway, and the extra storage would be great. I'd also add a peninsula to separate the kitchen from the breakfast nook, not just to give the space separation but so that you can do prep work on it and look out into the backyard at the same time." She shrugged. "That's all. Little changes."

Dylan bounded down the stairs, two at a time, landing on both feet at the bottom and grinning. "Everything's hooked up. You are wired."

"Thanks," Eric said. "I appreciate it. Is there enough room for your cot?"

"No problem."

"I'll be gone as of Friday, anyway," Marcy said. "He can take over the guest room."

A loud, awkward silence descended. When no one started up the conversation again, she stood. "I'm going to take a shower then go to bed."

"At nine o'clock?" Dylan asked.

"Now that the room is furnished, I can read in bed. Good time to study." She headed to the staircase. "There's a triple-berry pie in the refrigerator. Good night."

She heard a couple of mumbled good-nights in return, and then Eric's voice more clearly. "Have a seat, Dylan."

Marcy smiled to herself. She'd done what she'd intended. They were alone together, with little possibility of being interrupted.

If only her life could be directed so easily.

Chapter Eight

"You're different today," Eric said as Dylan sat in the chair across from him—or, rather, slouched in the chair.

"Yeah? Well, teenagers are moody."

Eric stifled a laugh. The kid had a pretty good sense of humor when he was in the mood to show it. "I remember. But being moody is one thing. Being rude is an entirely different matter."

"Who was I rude to?" He looked genuinely surprised.

"Annie."

"When?"

"She asked you questions. You ignored her."

"Oh, that." He shrugged. "She's nosy."

"She was just being friendly."

"For your sake, not mine."

Eric straightened. "What?"

"Come on, dude. Annie's got you in her sights. You're

like a buck in full antler the first day of hunting season."

Again, Eric stifled a laugh. "Let's say you're right, for the sake of argument, why does it matter to you? I thought you liked Annie."

"She's okay. Annie laughs a lot, but Marcy's more fun. And she really cares about me. She's trying to find me a job."

That was news to Eric. He let the idea settle for a few seconds. "Where?"

"At the place with the temporary jobs where she works."

"Doing what?"

"I don't know. Being a waiter or something. I have to be interviewed first. And get a new driver's license."

"So, you did have one at some point?"

"It got stolen. Then I didn't have an address to get a new one. Marcy's got a friend who says I can use her address." Dylan made eye contact, as if daring him to make the same offer.

"How's your arm?" Eric asked, noting the disappointment in Dylan's eyes. Maybe Marcy could be impetuous, but it wasn't Eric's style. As it was, he was housing the boy, feeding him, and paying him wages. He wasn't ready to leave him alone in the house—which presented a dilemma about what to do with him once Marcy left. He didn't want her to go, either. He'd gotten used to having people around—

"It's only stitches, man," Dylan said. "No one put me in the hospital for it. Give it up."

"I've seen you use it in ways you shouldn't. It needs time to heal. Let it rest."

"Yes, Dad." Dylan smirked.

"I've heard those same words in the same tone from my brothers and sister for years, and even from some students. Respect is a two-way street."

After a minute, Dylan nodded.

Eric decided the teenager had reached his limit of conversation—and he still hadn't revealed anything personal. Eric didn't know how he could help the boy without knowing what had put him on the streets in the first place.

He stood. "I'll get us some pie. Pick out a DVD, if you want."

Two hours, one galactic war, and forty explosions later, Dylan went to bed. Eric watched the news then went upstairs, too. Marcy had either fallen asleep with the light on or she was still awake.

He tapped lightly on her door but got no response. He tapped again. Nothing. He opened the door a crack. "Marcy?"

He pushed open the door a little more and saw her sleeping, her bedside lamp still on, her laptop open and leaning precariously. If she rolled over, it could slide right off and onto the floor.

Eric eased in, scooped up her computer and powered it down. He set it on the dresser then went back to turn out the lamp.

The sound of the click woke her up. She gasped, jolted straight up—

"It's just me," he said.

"What are you doing in here?"

She certainly got her wits about her in a hurry. "I knocked twice. I said your name. Then I rescued your laptop from disaster."

"Oh. Thank you."

She sat up and stretched, making him wish the light was still on. A streetlamp provided minimal illumination, enough for her hair to make a hazy cloud around her, as if she were part of a dream. His dream. He'd had plenty of those lately.

He sat on the side of her bed, facing her. She tugged the sheet up a little.

"Dylan told me everything—about the job, the DMV, your friend offering her address," Eric said.

"It wasn't a secret. I just hadn't had time to tell you."

"You should've talked to me before you took action. Marcy, as long as he's under my roof, he's my responsibility. Mine to take care of."

She cocked her head. "Do you plan to do that?"

"I'm already doing that. But here's the thing—if you get involved with him and it turns out he's got big problems, you're going to get caught up in them, too. Until he tells us about his past, he shouldn't be coddled."

"Who's coddling him? I offered to drive him to the DMV to replace his license. I offered to get him an interview with Julia for possible work."

"You also arranged for him to use your friend's address. You're making everything easy for him."

"I'm giving him a chance," she said, her voice rising. "I can't believe you'd be so callous as to stand by and let him stumble his way through life. You know what I've learned? Teenagers who are living on the streets usually end up as criminals. I'm trying to prevent that. He seems like a good kid. He's defensive and protective, but I think there must be reasons for that."

"I'm not being callous, Marcy. I'm trying to get him to do things on his own—which builds pride and self-respect. I won't let him go back to living on the streets, but he needs to figure some things out on his own and act on them. As for becoming a criminal, he's already proven that." He raised a hand when she started to interrupt. "He stole food. I know that's not a big deal. But there are so many programs in town where he can get food—and jobs, day jobs that could lead to something more permanent."

"Obviously our parenting methods are different. I think he needs a home first, a sense of security, then the rest can follow. He's already bonded with you."

"If that were true, he would've confided in me, trusted me to help. Look, we could go round and round about this with neither of us changing our minds. Let's just see how it goes for a few more days."

"He needs to get his driver's license or he's stuck completely. For that to happen, he needs an address."

"Let's agree we're at an impasse and let it go."

"I don't think we'll ever not be at an impasse. You are the most black-and-white person I've ever met. You have very little give."

"So are you."

"Me? In what way? I'm constantly giving in."

"No, you're not. You just go about things differently." He actually liked that about her. She was tenacious. He'd met too many women who gave in. He'd thought he was fine with that, that he was happy getting them to change their minds to his way of thinking—until he'd met Marcy. She didn't allow him to be complacent.

"When you're done with this semester and you have your AA degree, what's next?" he asked.

She drew up her knees and rested her arms across them. "You're quite the night owl, aren't you?"

He was stalling because he didn't want to go to bed.

He was tired of the single life, and she was good company. Lively company. He captured a lock of her hair and rubbed it between his fingers. "You're as evasive as Dylan."

"In what way?"

"I've asked you about your education a couple of times and your plans for the future, but you've never answered. Either you change the subject or ask me a question in return."

"I figured you were just making conversation. Anyway, it's almost midnight, Professor. I'm tired."

And she'd evaded his question again.

He gave up. "Too tired for this?" he asked instead. He moved in close, waited for her to object, and then he kissed her. Her arms came around him. She stroked his neck with her fingertips, the light scraping of her nails giving him chills.

She was wearing a tank top made of a touchably light and soft fabric, so that he could feel every bone as he trailed his fingers down her spine then slipped them under the fabric, stroking her smooth skin. Her mouth was warm and encouraging, gradually becoming more demanding.

He waited for his brain to caution him that this wasn't a good idea, but no such admonition came. He waited for her to stop him, even slow him down, but no denial came from her, either, just little sounds of appreciation.

He peeled her top off and tossed it aside. She arched as he stroked her breasts, enjoying the full weight of them, their firmness, and the silkiness of her skin. He let her nipples press into his palms before moving his thumbs over them, circling the hard flesh again and again, as she urged him to do more by arching farther, bringing herself closer.

She tasted like heaven, the scent of her fragrant skin filling his head. He felt her tug at his shirt and angled back so she could pull it up and over his head. He stretched out on top of her, the skin-to-skin sensation making him draw a sharp breath. He moved her legs apart with his and settled. She wrapped her legs around him and lifted her hips, making closer contact, agony and ecstasy, denial and pleasure. She was all woman, all curvy, soft yet firm, arousing. He liked how she smelled, how she tasted, how she looked. He liked how she responded to his every touch by digging her fingers into him or nipping his shoulder or intensifying their kiss.

He rolled to his side, taking her along, pulling her leg over his, gliding his hand over her rear, squeezing and cherishing. She angled back a little so that she could caress his chest, her fingertips dancing down his body. She unbuttoned and unzipped his shorts, making him groan.

"Better?" she asked.

"Much," he said, then caught his breath as she slid down him and pressed her lips to him through his briefs, her breath hot and moist. He clutched the sheets as she pulled the elastic waist down just far enough to touch him with her tongue, circling, swirling, taking the time to savor, to tease, to send him soaring. Almost, almost, almost....

The sound of a door opening reached them. They froze, listening to the creak of the floorboards. The bathroom door opened and closed.

"Since when do teenagers have to get up in the middle of the night?" he asked, almost growling the words.

She started to laugh, and pressed her mouth against his abdomen to block the sound—which didn't help him one bit. He'd been so close. He ached now, denied as he was.....

Neither of them moved until Dylan's bedroom door was shut again. Now what? They couldn't take things any further, nor could Eric leave the room while there was a chance Dylan could hear him.

"Maybe it was a sign," Marcy whispered, moving up, putting her head on the pillow opposite his, dragging the sheet over both of them.

"Of what?"

"That we weren't supposed to be doing what we were doing."

"I don't believe in signs. And I believe in finishing what I start."

She ran her fingers through his hair. "Maybe another time."

"Maybe?"

"Who knows what the future will bring." She softened the words with a kiss. She was torn between being disappointed and grateful they'd been interrupted. She couldn't seem to drum up any willpower to resist him, even when she knew the relationship couldn't go anywhere. They were opposites in so many ways. And while opposites may attract, they didn't necessarily stay together for the long haul.

Not that she was looking for the long haul. Nope. Not yet. And he seemed in a hurry to get to the long haul. To settle down and start having those kids he'd talked about wanting.

Marcy realized he'd fallen asleep, which presented a dilemma. Should she wake him up and send him on his way? Or—

Or, she decided. She might not get another opportunity for the *or.*

Her eyes drifted shut, then the next thing she knew, she was spooned against him, his arm across her waist, his hand resting under one breast. It was almost 6:00 a.m. Although Dylan didn't generally get up before eight, Marcy wanted Eric gone long before then. Like *now.* Before she gave in to his sexual pull again.

She felt him wake up with a start, his hand jerking upward then slowly, carefully resettling. He spooned a little closer, too, tucking his knees more tightly against hers. Should she pretend to be asleep? Maybe he would just slip out of bed and disappear. That would be the easiest on both of them.

But just then he pushed her hair aside and kissed her shoulder. He moved his hand slowly over her breasts until her nipples were hard, then he slid lower, much lower, under her pajama bottoms, to stroke her lightly again and again. She arched to meet his hand, tightened when he slipped a finger inside her, then protested when he pulled his hand away and rolled out of bed.

She dropped onto her back, staring at him in disbelief. He was going to leave her like this? All hot and wanting?

He kissed her. "Maybe another time," he whispered, looking her over, then he left, quietly, carefully.

Smugly.

After a minute she laughed. She liked clever. He was definitely clever. She liked sexy, too, and he was that in spades.

Maybe another time.

No maybe about it, Marcy thought. The only question now was *when?*

Anticipation was one of the pleasures of life. Knowing a gift was coming but not knowing when, heightened the senses.

Unless, of course, the gift never arrived at all.

Then it all became one big regret for a missed opportunity.

Chapter Nine

Marcy kept herself busy in the kitchen when Eric came down the stairs a while later. She wondered how to act now that they'd slept together—without "sleeping" together. How would it change their relationship? Because it was certainly bound to.

She heard him come into the kitchen, but she didn't turn around from where she was washing grapes, instead she waited, nervous and excited, for him to make the first move. Dylan was in the shower, so they were assured some alone time.

"Good morning," Eric said as he picked up the coffee pot and poured himself a mug.

"Same to you," she said, sensing him moving closer. Would he kiss her? Give her a hug? Tease her a little?

"About Dylan," he said.

Startled, she met his gaze but couldn't form a sentence. No kiss? No hug?

"Please don't let him use your friend's address for the DMV, or anything else, for that matter. I meant it when I said that while he's under my roof, he's my responsibility. I'll deal with it. With him."

Marcy found her voice. "How am I supposed to take back the offer? I'm sure he's counting on it."

"I'll tell him myself. He'll probably be angry, but it'll be directed at me, not you."

Annoyed at his interference, she went back to her task, then felt him slide his hand down her hair.

"Good morning," he said in an entirely different tone of voice, a sexy one. *Big mistake,* she thought. *You should've led with that instead of the parental one.*

"Morning," she said, moving out of range to get dishes and silverware.

A short, tense silence ensued.

"Thank you for all the wonderful meals you've prepared. I appreciate the extra effort you've taken, and I know Dylan does, too."

"I love to cook, and I also need to feel like I'm earning my keep." She brushed past him to set the table. "I'm mostly a glorified babysitter, after all."

There was another long stretch of silence. "Are you mad at me?" he asked.

What was your first clue, Sherlock? She heard the shower turn off in the upstairs bathroom, which meant Dylan would join them in a few minutes, and there were things she needed to say, especially based on how he'd treated her this morning, a clear indicator of how life would be, if she let it go on this way, *his* way.

"Last night was a mistake," she said. "It can't happen again."

"Why?"

"I don't have time for a relationship right now."

"We both know what would've happened if we hadn't been interrupted."

"Maybe. Maybe not. The fact is, it didn't happen. I know you don't believe in signs, Eric, but I do. And this one is lit up on a Jumbotron for me."

The timer went off, meaning her oven omelet needed cheese sprinkled on top.

"You're not thinking logically," he said. "You're—"

"Hold on. Just hold on. What you mean is, I'm not thinking with the same logic that you are. Well, guess what? I'm allowed my own logic, which isn't always just-the-facts-ma'am, but emotion. I know myself. I know how long it takes me to recover from—" *a broken heart* "—disappointment. I'll be gone in a couple of days. Let's just keep our distance until then, okay? I've never denied there's a physical attraction between us, but it's what we do about it that counts."

She knew she was all but shoving him into Annie's open arms, but Marcy had to stay true to herself, her short-term education goals, and her long-term life plan.

Eric didn't have a response, so he took his mug onto the back deck and sat in a newly delivered lounge chair. Ever since he'd left her room that morning, she was all he could think about. He wasn't usually one to obsess. She'd become an obsession. He was bewildered by it, appalled at it—and appreciative of it.

She continued to be a force of nature in his life, unafraid to contradict him, able to go toe-to-toe.... And yet there was a soft side to her, vulnerable and nurturing. She called him paternal. Well, she was maternal. They made an interesting team.

He heard Dylan's voice, then the screen door opened. "Breakfast is ready."

"Thanks. Step out here for a minute, please."

Dylan stuffed his hands in his pockets and came up beside Eric.

"How would you like to go to work with me today?"

"To do what?"

"Hang out. The content of the class may not interest you, but I think you'd enjoy seeing the campus. Class itself is only an hour and forty minutes. You wouldn't have to sit still for long."

"Okay. I guess."

Eric stood.

"Just so you don't get your hopes up," Dylan said before they went into the kitchen. "College isn't for me."

"Why not?"

"I want to be a mechanic. Want to own my own auto shop someday."

Ah. A tidbit of information. It was a start. "I'm glad to hear you have a goal."

"Since I was a kid," Dylan said, his expression serious.

Eric nodded. "I get that. I always wanted to teach. If you have a passion for something, it's much easier to accomplish it."

Marcy was seated at the table waiting for them.

"I'm going to work with Eric today," Dylan said.

"That sounds interesting." She scooped salsa onto her omelet.

"You're welcome to come along," Eric said. "Maybe

you could transfer to Davis when you're done at Sac City College."

"I'll be going to Sac State University," she said. "I've already applied."

"What's your major?" Dylan asked.

Eric tried not to smile. He figured she wouldn't refuse to answer the question, even though she'd withheld the answer from him.

She seemed to sigh slightly. "Business administration, with a marketing minor."

"Seriously?" Eric asked, surprised. He clamped his mouth shut when she shot daggers at him with her eyes.

"You have a problem with that?"

Before he could answer, Dylan spoke again. "What do you want to do?"

"I haven't decided. I figure the classes will help narrow down that decision for me."

"So, you don't have a passion for anything in particular?"

Eric smiled at Dylan's prodding—and his choice of words, repetitious of Eric's a minute ago.

"A passion?" Marcy repeated.

"You know, business is a big field."

"I know, but that's part of the education process— to discover where your interests and strengths are by learning," Marcy said.

"I would've pegged you for something involving taking care of people," Dylan said. "You're good at that. A teacher, maybe. Or even a chef."

"Or a flight attendant?" she asked.

He cocked his head. "For sure."

"I was one, years ago. I loved it."

"Why'd you quit?" Dylan asked.

"I didn't. I got laid off, along with a whole lot of other people. Then when they wanted to hire me back, it would've meant a move to the east coast. I needed to stay here." Her voice trailed off.

Eric exchanged a look with Dylan. What had happened that made her stay in Sacramento? "Marketing is about manipulation," Eric said. "You're way too direct for that."

That got a smile out of her. "For better or for worse." She toasted him with her mug.

"What will you do while we're gone today?" Eric asked.

"Probably lie on the couch, eat truffles and watch the Food Network."

Eric laughed. A few seconds later, Dylan realized it was a joke and laughed, too. They were having a good morning, like a family eating breakfast together before starting their day. Eric hadn't known what to expect from Marcy after last night, and had tread carefully at first, not bringing it up until they'd talked about something else first so that she wouldn't think he only had sex on his mind.

Which he did. He'd tried to be sensitive, but somehow he'd irritated her instead. In the light of day she must be regretting what happened.

He wasn't. Not one bit. He'd do it again—although hopefully with a different outcome—tonight, if she was willing.

"Can you be ready in ten minutes?" he asked Dylan. "I'm getting a haircut before I head to school."

"Think I could get one today, too?" He ran a hand over his hair. Although clean, it was chopped up pretty badly.

"Probably. Won't know until we get there."

Dylan pushed away from the table. "I'll be back in a few."

"You were quite subtle," Marcy said, looking at Eric over her coffee mug. "Well done."

"He needs to be making his own decisions, even if it's just about haircuts."

"Even if they're your decisions." She smiled. "It's a useful parenting technique."

"Well honed through plenty of mistakes, believe me. I did a lot of ordering around of my siblings in the first couple of years before I realized there were more effective ways to get them to do what I wanted."

"Apparently you could have a career in marketing." She smiled sweetly.

He laughed. He realized he'd been doing that a lot since he met her. "Touché."

She would be leaving tomorrow, and these mornings sharing a meal and conversation would end. Consequently, so would the laughter, unless Dylan upped his game in that regard.

Eric watched Marcy take her empty plate to the sink. She wore her usual outfit of tank top and shorts, neither of which was overly tight. But now he knew what she looked like without the top, without the bra. He knew the taste and texture of her nipples, and the weight of her breasts resting in his hands. He'd never been much of a breast man, so he didn't understand why he was so focused on them now. Give him a nice rear to look at, however—

He stopped the thought. She had that, too. Actually, she had it all and then some.

He had one chance left—tonight. And she didn't seem to be of the same mindset.

He needed to change that.

Eric carried his plate to the kitchen counter, reaching around her to set it in the sink, lightly pressing his chest against her back, his arm brushing hers. She went still.

"Thank you for breakfast," he said.

She didn't say anything at first. Not *you're welcome.* Not *back off.*

Then, "Is this how you keep your distance, Eric?"

"I didn't agree to."

"Your silence implied it."

"My silence meant I was thinking it over. In thinking it over, I realized I can't keep my hands off you."

"Then I guess it's a good thing I'm leaving tomorrow." She turned to face him. He didn't move. "Maybe I'll leave today instead. There's really nothing left for me to do. You don't work on Fridays, anyway, so you'll be home for Dylan."

His plan had backfired with all the subtlety of a cannon firing. "Don't go."

"This isn't easy for me, either," she said, low and harsh. "But to borrow Robert Frost's famous words, I have 'miles to go before I sleep.' You're eleven years older than me, Eric. You've accomplished what you set out to do. I'm still on my journey."

"And sleeping with me would interfere with that? How?"

Marcy heard a hint of desperation in his voice. She couldn't remember being wanted as much as he wanted her. She didn't think it was proximity that was driving him, but an attraction that would've happened no matter where or how they'd met.

Lust at first sight. They'd both agreed about that.

He kissed her, softly, persuasively, breaking down her determination. "Tonight?" he whispered against her lips.

As so often had happened, Dylan came thundering down the stairs then.

Eric put some distance between them. His eyes twinkled merrily. She was glad he'd kept a sense of humor about the interruption.

"It's a simple yes or no question, Marcy."

"Maybe."

He laughed.

Dylan looked from Eric to Marcy, curiosity in his gaze. "How short do you think I should get my hair cut?" he asked her. "You know, for jobs."

"Any length is popular now. Do what suits you. You've got some natural wave. Women love that."

He automatically touched his hair. "They do?"

"That and a great smile, which you also have. You could work on your communication skills a little."

"She starts with flattery then comes the zinger." He grinned. "I'm on to you."

"Let's go," Eric said.

Dylan said goodbye then headed out the kitchen door, the nearest access to the driveway. Eric sauntered sexily behind, but stopped to have the last word. "Think of me."

"I think I'll read ahead in my psychology book to the chapter called 'Sexual Addiction.'"

His smile was slow and tempting. "An addict is someone who doesn't have the ability to manage or control their addiction. In that sense it's true about me," he said, "but only around *you*. So what does that make it? Have a good day."

Marcy waited for the car to back out then plopped into a chair. Whew! The man was all fire and temptation. She never would've guessed the mathematics professor was a romantic, but he sure did know which buttons of hers to push. The right words uttered in the right tone of voice had turned up her thermostat to its boiling point.

Barely a minute had passed after Eric and Dylan left when the doorbell rang. Marcy looked through the peephole and saw Annie with Lucy perched on her hip. Marcy opened the door.

"I know this is a total cliché," Annie said, wearing a hopeful expression and carrying a measuring cup. "But may I borrow a cup of sugar?"

"Of course. Come in." They headed to the kitchen. "How are you, Miss Lucy?"

The toddler looked down, a finger in her mouth, her smile around it sweet.

"What are you making?" Marcy asked.

"Peach pie. So, I saw Dylan leaving with Eric."

"It's take-your-kid-to-work day," Marcy said.

Annie frowned. Marcy almost shook her head. The woman had zero sense of humor. Marcy wondered, not for the first time, what Annie and Eric talked about when they were alone, which had happened a few times during the week, at Annie's invitation, but also at Marcy's urging, something she was regretting.

"I'm kidding," Marcy said, reaching for the container of sugar. "Dylan tagged along for the day, that's all. He's getting antsy, waiting for his arm to heal."

"So, he'll be around for a while?" Annie asked, moseying to the kitchen window.

"Eric promised him the backyard cleanup is his."

"And what about you? Are you staying on?"

Ah ha. The real reason why Annie had stopped by. "Tomorrow's my last day."

Annie turned around. "I'll miss you."

Sure you will. If Annie hadn't been holding Lucy, she would've been rubbing her hands together in anticipation of having Eric to herself. The weird thing was, Marcy really liked the woman. They might've become friends under different circumstances.

"Although it's kind of open-ended," Marcy added. "He'll probably need me now and then."

"I'll remind him that his new neighbors are always willing to help each other," Annie said. "We're all friendly, here."

Marcy handed her the full measuring cup. "Yes, I've noticed how friendly you are."

Even though Marcy kept her tone of voice pleasant, Annie didn't pretend to misunderstand.

"Men like Eric don't come along often," she said. "My late husband didn't take life too seriously, and it led to a lot of problems before and after his death. Eric seems responsible."

"I would say that's an accurate description. You're lucky you have a career, though. You won't have to struggle to take care of yourself and your daughter."

"My goal is to be home with Lucy until she starts school, even though it's a sacrifice. Eric agrees I'm doing the right thing. He strongly believes in the stay-at-home mom."

Her quoting Eric made Marcy uncomfortable. "My

mom did that, too. Well, have fun baking your pie," she said to Lucy, more than just a hint to Annie that she should leave.

"Thanks so much," Annie said.

Marcy shut the door behind them, their conversation running through her head. She agreed that men like Eric didn't come along often. If he made a commitment to someone or something, he would follow through, no matter what. She was sure of that.

But Annie's comment that he strongly believed in the stay-at-home mom was yet another indicator of how far apart they were on life issues. Marcy didn't disagree about the value of children having a stay-at-home parent, but she'd also had it hammered home that she needed a career to fall back on for when life changed—and it was bound to, in one way or another. Lori was her biggest example and motivator, and more recently Shana. And even Marcy's mother had pushed Marcy toward a college education all her life, and a career.

With those thoughts buzzing around in her head, she headed to the laundry room, wanting to be all caught up before she left tomorrow. While she sorted the clothes she found her eyes welling up.

"This is crazy," she said out loud. They weren't her family. She wasn't leaving them. She was just finishing a job she'd been paid to do.

She leaned against the washer. Who was she kidding? Eric and Dylan had stopped being a job to her, maybe they'd *never* been a job. She'd been sympathetic to Dylan from the moment he'd ridden his bike into the backyard and asked for work.

As for Eric—he and she might think differently about life, but she respected him. The thought of leaving hurt. But the thought of leaving after she'd made love with him?

In the end, there was no decision to be made about whether she would sleep with him tonight. Based on her reasoned logic, which she figured Eric would admire if he knew, the decision made itself.

Now she only had to tell him.

Chapter Ten

"Do you want to stop at the DMV?" Eric asked Dylan as they left the campus parking lot.

It took him a few seconds to answer. "Marcy said she'd take me."

"I'm aware of that, but if you want to use my address, then I need to go with you."

Dylan's surprise was palpable. "I can use your address?"

"I won't be moving anytime soon. Marcy's friend lives in an apartment. You'd have to keep track of her to know if you need to make changes."

"Thanks, man."

Eric pulled into the DMV parking lot a few minutes later.

"Thanks for doing this," Dylan said. "And for taking me with you today. It was cool watching you teach.

You're kinda different from at home. Kinda like you're putting on a show. You're not Eric. You're Professor Sheridan."

"Being aware of who your audience is and then acting accordingly is one of the most important skills you can develop."

"Isn't that sorta like faking?"

"Not at all. You're adapting to whatever the situation is. You can be flexible and still be true to yourself."

Dylan looked out the windshield. "My dad was rigid."

"Was?"

"Is. Is rigid."

"I thought that about my dad, too," Eric said. "Years later I came to realize he hadn't been rigid so much as consistent—to a fault, maybe. I didn't learn how to compromise because he never did."

"You turned out okay."

Eric smiled. "Thanks. Through a great deal of trial and error, and having brothers and a sister who wouldn't let me 'turn into Dad,' as they put it. Or Mom, for that matter."

"What was she like?" Dylan asked.

"Organized. Driven. She was an attorney, a public defender. She was a little more flexible than Dad, but not by much."

"My mom never worked. And she was a softie."

"Was?"

Dylan swallowed. "Was."

Eric clamped a hand on his shoulder. Something they had in common.

Two girls walked by the car, laughing. Dylan straightened and looked around. "Guess we should get going," he said. "Marcy will wonder where we are."

"You know she's leaving tomorrow, don't you?"

"I know she's got a job house-sitting. That sounds kinda cool. She said she's taken care of all kinds of places, from mansions all the way down to mobile homes. Usually people have pets. She likes that, too. She moves around too much, so she can't have a pet of her own."

Obviously, Marcy and Dylan had different kinds of conversations than he had with the boy. Eric hadn't heard any of this. He opened the car door and got out. "She's a pretty interesting person. Very independent."

Dylan eyed him as they walked toward the building. "I think that gets to you. You guys clash sometimes."

"I'm not used to someone in my employ disagreeing with me."

Dylan laughed. "Hm. That sounds pretty *rigid* to me. Are you sure you've changed?"

Eric didn't know what to say to that. Yes, he'd changed. Ask any of his siblings.

But had he changed enough?

While standing beside Dylan at the counter, Eric learned his real last name—Vargas—and his former address. Not familiar with Sacramento, Eric didn't have a clue where it was.

When it came time to pay for the replacement card, Eric crossed his arms until the transaction was done. It would be easy to foot the bill, but Dylan wouldn't take on the responsibility he needed to if Eric made it too easy. Dylan had earned his wages. He could pay his own expenses.

Soon they were on their way, Dylan's temporary license tucked into a pouch he carried around his neck. He looked happy, even overjoyed. Eric understood. Driving meant independence—if you had a car.

At the house, Eric hadn't even turned off the engine before Dylan was out of the car and flying to the back door, calling Marcy's name. No teenage cool for him this time.

Marcy was grinning at Dylan's enthusiasm.

"Have you started dinner?" Eric asked.

"Not yet."

"I think we should go out, the three of us."

"Why?" she asked.

"It's your last night. We haven't had time to talk much, just the three of us."

"We talk all the time," she said, confused.

Dylan crossed his arms, his change of mood abrupt. "You're not getting it, Marcy. See, I let him in on my past a little and now he wants more. He figures if we're in public, I'll be all polite and everything."

Eric shifted from one foot to the other, the truth of Dylan's accusation hitting home. Not that he would admit it. "How do you get that out of inviting you to dinner?"

"Reading you is like reading a book, man. Marcy's even easier."

"Hold on," Marcy said. "How did I get caught up in this?"

"You ask little questions about my past—"

"Which you don't answer."

Dylan's expression went dark. "Maybe there's a good reason for that."

"I wouldn't know."

Eric was about to stop the discussion before it escalated into a situation they all regretted, and which might make Dylan feel forced to leave. But Dylan exploded, his shift from happy to angry so sudden it was baffling. Maybe he'd just been holding it in.

"What do you wanna hear?" he asked, his tone chilling. "How my mother didn't want me so I ended up in foster care when I was six? How my foster mom died in January and my dad kicked me out the day after graduation?" He walked away, stiff-legged. "Would you like to hear about the shelters I tried to live in? How someone stole stuff from me, but no one believed me. Or the guy who made moves on me? I never went back there either. It was…safer on the streets. You name it, I've slept there. Parks, building alcoves, here, of course."

"Dylan," Marcy said, moving toward him.

"Stop right there. You wanted to know. You have to listen. I learned where every handout was given, showed up at all of them, even the places that just give snacks. What I really missed was showers. Didn't get a shower very often, just cleaned up at public restrooms. Every once in a while I'd get work for a day, but that's really competitive. I had to hide and then rush out when someone would come looking for people. A couple of the men got to know me, knew I worked hard, and they'd look for me."

He spoke to Eric. "Your house wasn't the most comfortable place to stay. It was really hot, and I didn't dare open a lot of windows, even at night, but it was safe. I could sleep straight through the night without keeping one eye open. You don't know how good that felt."

"Did you grieve for your mom?" Marcy asked quietly.

"No. Yes. A little." His voice was raspy. "Dad didn't,

so I couldn't. Couldn't even talk about her. I just keep thinking how mad she'd be if she knew he'd kicked me out. And sometimes…"

He tunneled his fingers through his newly cut hair, then locked his hands behind his head. "Sometimes I wish he'd died instead. We could've managed, Mom and me. Is that what you wanted to hear?" Heartbreak coated every word.

He ran away, raced upstairs, slammed his bedroom door.

Flashback after flashback flared in Eric's mind. Fury had been Eric's companion for a long time after his parents died, too. He had been left much better off financially than the boy, but he hadn't had time to grieve, either. He'd had to be strong and responsible at a time in his life when most people were discovering freedom and independence.

He'd fought breaking down in front of anyone, as well. It hadn't helped, no matter what he'd been told about how it would make him feel better. He was better when he kept things to himself.

Still, he had no regrets. His brothers and sister were happy and productive. That was what mattered.

He could hear Marcy crying. He didn't want to comfort her, as heartless as that sounded. He was feeling too raw himself. Comforting her might open his own floodgates.

So, he gripped her shoulder for a second then climbed the stairs to Dylan's room. He knocked but didn't wait for a response. Dylan was lying face down on his cot.

Eric crouched beside him. "I know that was hard, but I'm glad you told us. I'm really sorry you lost your mom. I do know how that feels."

Dylan stayed silent.

"Here's what I'm proposing, if it meets your approval," Eric said. "Apparently you should rest your arm for another few days before you do any serious hard labor, so during that time you need to go out and look for work. When you get a job, I'll help you find a good used car, for which I will loan you the money to buy it, and for insurance, as well."

Dylan lifted his head. "Are you serious?"

Eric nodded. "We'll have a contract, and you will pay me back at a rate that's manageable for you. You can continue to live here for now. I'm going to leave that part open-ended and see how things go. In return for room and board, you'll do the yard work, your own laundry and help out with the cleaning. Do you cook?"

"Nothing you'd probably want to eat."

He smiled. "Maybe we'll take some classes. Otherwise, we're going to have a brand-new beautiful kitchen with no one to use it." He leaned forward. "The goal here, Dylan, is for you to become independent. If I learn a few things along the way, like learn to cook, that's good, too."

"Thank you."

"You're welcome. I'll leave you alone now. I just wanted to ease your mind a little."

He went downstairs and found Marcy curled up in a chair.

"Is he okay?"

"He will be." He decided she didn't look at all like the she-bear she frequently was when it came to Dylan—his champion.

"What are you smiling about?" she asked.

He sat across from her. "You."

She folded her hands in her lap. "That will probably change when I tell you my decision about tonight."

His fingers dug into the chair arms. "I take it you'll be locking your door."

"Figuratively, anyway."

He was unprepared for the blow of her refusal. "Why?"

"For a whole lot of really good reasons."

"That you're not going to share?"

"We already discussed them this morning, Eric. To be fair, I did give it more thought while you were gone. My reasons didn't change."

"So, you're fine leaving things unfinished?" he asked. "With not knowing what we would be like together?"

"I have to be fine with my decision." She stood and looked around, as if she didn't know where she was. "I need to go for a walk. Oh, by the way, Annie stopped by this morning. She's ready, willing and able to take over for me. Sounds like she's a pretty good cook, too."

Eric didn't move from his chair after she left. It was a pretty good indicator of her state of mind that she didn't remember to take her cell phone, which she'd set on the coffee table earlier. She'd needed to escape in a hurry. Why? Was she afraid he would try to change her mind?

He knew how to take no for answer, although the way he'd kept coming at her this morning might not have been a good indicator of that. What he needed to do now was get through the next twenty-four hours or so without bringing it up again and making her uncomfortable.

After that she would be gone, all temptation removed,

and he would have plenty to keep him busy. Work, kitchen renovation, Dylan. His friendly neighbors.

Annie. Who dropped in without notice and needed to be prodded out the door to get her to leave.

Well, he'd wanted a life change. He'd certainly gotten what he wished for.

The next day, Marcy packed up her car early so that when the time came to leave, she could just get in her car and go. She'd washed her sheets and remade the guest bed for Dylan. She'd left a meat loaf and potato salad in the refrigerator for dinner. Eric had a lunch meeting with the chair of his department, but was expected home well before Marcy had to leave.

Dylan was in the backyard trying to pull weeds left-handed, and only occasionally swore loud enough for Marcy to hear through the open windows.

She felt at a loss. She would be leaving in an hour and a half, and everything was done, so she went outside to talk with Dylan as he worked. Distraction usually lessened burdens—in this case, for both of them, although entirely different burdens. She was already feeling the loss of Eric and Dylan in her life.

As she approached, Dylan looked up and smiled, sweat dripping down his face. He grabbed the towel he'd brought with him and dragged it down his face and chest. "I'll be glad when summer's over," he said. "And when I can use my other arm."

"You must be feeling pretty good about everything else, though."

He shrugged.

"I wrote down my cell-phone number and left it on your bed. If you want me to pick you up and take you to At Your Service sometime this week, let me know. Those kinds of jobs we talked about are usually in the evening or on weekends."

"How do I get into the house-sitting business?"

"Word of mouth. I started with one client several years ago. Now I have about twenty regulars. They know I get booked up, so they reserve me early."

"What happens if you can't do it?"

"Some clients have backups. Others use At Your Service, although it's a little more expensive, with the agency fees. I like it because I'm generally free during the days to take on other temp jobs, so I'm making double pay, plus I keep my independence instead of bunking with Lori and the kids. You really think it's something you'd like to do?"

"I'm kinda happy living here right now, but maybe in a few months? Maybe you could recommend me?"

"We'll see how it goes. I—" Her cell phone rang. "Excuse me," she said to Dylan and then, seeing who was calling, answered the call, a smile spreading across her face.

"Hello, Mr. Gianelli."

"Who're you calling Mister, darling girl?"

"My favorite client." He was, too, and not just because he stocked his refrigerator with incredible meals he prepared in advance, and arranged for his regular massage therapist to show up on Tuesday evening just for her.

He laughed. "Excellent answer."

"I hope nothing's wrong. Are the kitties okay?" She wasn't sure if she wanted him to cancel on her. And if so, would she tell Eric?

"The boys are as sweet as ever, but pretty, pretty please could you come at two o'clock instead of three?"

It would mean leaving here in twenty minutes. Eric had expected to be home by now, so she should be able to say goodbye in person. Regardless, she couldn't turn down her favorite client. "Sure, Brutie. What's up?"

"The dishwasher conked out. The store said they could replace it this afternoon, if that's okay."

"No problem. As long as they expect to be done by five-thirty so I can get to work on time."

"They promised."

Marcy laughed.

"I know, I know. Well, if they show up too late, just reschedule. See you in a little bit."

She pushed the end button and tucked the phone in her pocket.

"You're leaving early?" Dylan asked.

"At one-thirty."

"What if Eric isn't home by then?" He sat back, gripping the hand weeder and frowning at her. "You should let him know."

She started to argue then got out her phone instead and dialed Eric. It went to voice mail. "Hi, it's Marcy. My client just called and wants me an hour early, so I'll be leaving pretty soon. I didn't want you to come home and be surprised that I'm already gone. Call me if you aren't— Well, either way, call me, please." She put the phone away.

"You like him, don't you?" Dylan asked.

"He's a kind and decent person. Of course I like him."

"More than that."

"What's your point, Dylan?"

His voice dropped. "Without you around, Annie will come over a lot more."

"I thought you liked Annie."

"She leaves Lucy alone in the house. That drives me crazy."

Marcy, too. She hated it, in fact. "She's got the baby monitor, and an alarm, and the dog."

"I get that. It's just wrong."

Marcy kept her phone in her hand, an eye on the time. Eric didn't call. She assumed he'd turned his phone off for the lunch meeting, which was probably lasting longer than he'd expected.

Maybe it was for the best. Leaving would be much harder with him there.

When she couldn't wait a second later, she hugged Dylan goodbye, tears blinding her. He squeezed her extra hard, too. "Everything Eric does is because he cares about you," Marcy said, pulling back.

"I know. But I gotta be myself, too. I've been making my own way. He needs to remember I'm different from him. And his brothers and sister."

"Give him time."

"I'm not going anywhere," he said with a grin, making it easier for her to drive away.

Hours later, Eric still hadn't called her back. She started her shift at Score, was grateful for the usual Saturday night of full capacity and rowdy customers watching a variety of sporting events. She rarely had a second to think, much less wallow. Maybe because she'd turned him down last night, he'd decided to cut ties completely.

"Guy at table twenty-six is asking for you," her co-worker Brittany said. "New beau?"

Marcy spotted Eric in the far corner, watching her steadily. She melted. It seemed like days since she'd seen him, not hours. She wanted to run to him, to fly into his arms, to be held close and tight.

Instead she walked to his table, getting stopped by customers a couple of times, but continuing to her destination after fielding requests.

"Hi," she said.

He pushed something across the table. "You forgot your key."

She'd left it on his dresser. "Job's done."

"I'd prefer you keep it. That way if I need you, we won't have the logistics of how to get you a key."

She looked at it but didn't pick it up. "If you need me?"

"Or you need me. Or a place to stay between housesitting jobs." He scooped up the key and held it out. "Take it. Please."

Marcy slipped it into her pocket, her hand shaking. "Is there something I can get you?"

He gave her a long, thorough look, then leaned back in his chair. "Whatever's on tap."

"You got it." She walked away wondering what he really wanted.

And if she would ever find out.

Chapter Eleven

Eric watched Marcy scoop up a few empty pitchers as she headed toward the bar. She moved gracefully. He'd noticed that about her before—her economy of movement, which was at odds with her vibrant personality.

Score seemed like a good fit for her. Located in the lobby of the Treetop Hotel in downtown Sacramento, it had a multitude of television screens mounted on the walls. Most sets were tuned to the Giants/Dodgers game being played in Los Angeles, which was tied in the bottom of the ninth inning.

Eric had been a Red Sox fan since birth, so he didn't pay much attention to the televisions.

Marcy returned with his tall glass of beer. "You're out late," she said.

It was ten o'clock. In New York, things would just

be heating up. "I took a nap. Old guys like me need to do that, you know."

She smiled at his joke. "Is everything okay?" she asked. "Dylan?"

"Everything is fine. I just needed to get out of the house."

"You left him alone?"

"He's eighteen, Marcy." Not that he hadn't been nervous about it, but he had to start trusting the kid sometime.

"Of course." She looked around the room quickly. "Um, as you can see we're really busy. What else can I get you? Are you hungry?"

Yes. For you. "What do you recommend?"

"Knowing your tastes run to the gourmet, I'd recommend the Gut-Buster Nachos."

He laughed, relaxing for the first time all evening. "If you say so."

"You got it."

She sashayed away. He noticed he wasn't the only man watching her, but he was pleased when she sneaked a peek at him, and only him, as she entered his order into the computer behind the bar. After that she disappeared into what he assumed was the kitchen, coming out with a large tray of food orders for a rowdy table of eight. She showed incredible strength and balance.

A little while later she brought his nachos, a spicy mound that he and Dylan together couldn't have finished, even with Dylan's healthy appetite. Gut-Buster, indeed.

Throughout the evening she stopped by his table now and then, but he didn't detain her, seeing how busy she was. He spent his time torn between being fascinated and jealous, an unfamiliar emotion. She handled the mostly male patrons with ease. Only one guy got overly friendly, sliding his arm around her waist. She said something that had him dropping his arm right away then looking nervously over his shoulder to where Eric was sitting. Eric decided to lift his glass in a toast, earning a blown kiss from Marcy, and hoots and hollers from the rest of the men at the table.

At twelve-fifteen the bartender shouted, "Last call" to the thirteen customers left. Marcy came up to his table. "Anything else?"

"Just the bill."

When she brought it, he didn't even open the folder but stood and handed her some bills. "What'd you say to the guy who put his arm around you?" he asked.

"I told him my boyfriend was sitting in the corner watching his every move. Thanks for playing along."

"My pleasure. What's your usual course of action if you don't have a boyfriend in the room?"

She pulled a laminated photograph from her back pocket. "This is Brutus Gianelli and me. He's a six-foot-five, two-hundred-and-ninety-pound defensive end when I need him to be."

"And is he a football player?"

"He's an opera singer. Which doesn't mean he isn't tough. He is. But I don't think he tackles. It's his house I'm watching this week."

Silence fell between them, not exactly awkward, but not comfortable, either.

After a few seconds, he cupped her shoulder. "See you," he said.

"Bye," Marcy managed to say when he was almost out the door, his brief touch still warm. She still had no idea why he'd come, unless it really was just to give her back the key. Or get out of the house, as he'd also said.

When she reached her car in the underground parking lot, she found Eric standing next to it. She didn't say a word, just walked up to him and kissed him. Having him watching her all night had been oddly like foreplay, and she couldn't wait a minute longer to touch him.

It didn't take him more than a millisecond to get caught up in the moment. "Can we go somewhere?" he asked against her mouth.

"To the house where I'm working. We can talk."

"Talk," he repeated.

She ran a finger across his lips. "Follow me."

"On your tail," he said, cupping her rear and pulling her against him for a few seconds.

She had fifteen minutes to think things over as she drove to Brutus's house, with Eric following close behind her. Fear and excitement battled inside her as she pulled into the garage. Not fear of him but herself and what she might lose if she got more deeply involved with him. She couldn't remember ever being in such turmoil over a man. It was especially disconcerting because she'd known him so briefly—and yet, it felt like forever.

She walked to the door connecting to the kitchen, then waited for him to join her.

"Do you really want to talk?" he asked. "I think you want the same thing I do, and it doesn't include complete sentences."

"How can you be so sure?"

"Because you took my key back. And because your hand was shaking when you did. It was all I needed to know." He cupped her cheek, ran his thumb across it.

"When I got to my car after my lunch this afternoon and found you'd left without …" He didn't finish the sentence. "I don't know how this is going to turn out anymore than you do, but I know we need to do something about the attraction that's taken over."

Marcy pushed the garage-door button, closing it. She grabbed the doorknob behind her and turned it. Two fluffy gray cats bounded across the kitchen to greet her. "Tom and Baby," she said to Eric, who didn't even give them a glance.

"Where's your room?"

"Upstairs, to the right."

He took her hand. They climbed the stairs together. She struggled to breathe. She shook.

She craved.

At the top of the stairs, she grabbed his other hand as well and walked backward, admiring him, more excited than she could ever remember being. The world could collapse around them, and it wouldn't stop what had been set into motion.

Marcy backed into the guest room and stopped by the bed. "I'm glad you're here," she said. "Glad you took action."

He framed her face with his hands, and then he kissed her in a way he never had before, brushing his lips delicately across hers, making her reach for more. She went up on tiptoe, trying to get closer. He kept his hands on her face, tipping her head the other way, only slightly deepening the kiss, sweeping her lower lip with his tongue lightly but thoroughly. She groaned, clutched his shirt in her fists and lifted it free so she could slide her hands underneath. His skin burned hot.

"I can't wait any longer," she said.

He smiled. "What's your rush?" he asked against her mouth. "Just enjoy it."

"I'm too wound up."

He moved her hand to cover the front of his jeans. "You think I'm not?"

"I want you inside me." The words came out more like an order.

"I'll be there. I promise."

Oh, he was enjoying this, tormenting her. Well, two could play that game. She pushed up his shirt, then used her tongue to trace a wet trail down his chest, slowly, enticingly, his stomach muscles twitching and contracting. She dipped her tongue behind his waistband, working the button with her fingers at the same time, popping it open, the zipper sliding apart. She pressed her mouth to him, breathed hot air through his sexy white briefs, then found herself pulled upright.

"How did you end up taking charge?" he asked, nipping her lips.

"You were too slow."

He laughed, low and appreciatively. "Well, maybe we *should* just get this over with the first time."

The first time. The words danced magically in her mind.

"What the hell?" he said. "How many pillows are on this bed, anyway?"

"Fourteen, I think."

"Ridiculous." Pillow after pillow hit the wall, the floor and the dresser, then Eric yanked back the layers of bedding until only the sheet remained. He turned to face Marcy again, slowed himself down just a little. "Do you have any idea what it was like for me watching you work tonight? I know what your breasts look like, feel like." He pulled her T-shirt over her head and tossed it aside. "I could picture you moving topless around the bar." He ran his fingertips along the edge of her bra. "Men stare at you when you're not looking. Do you know that?"

She made some kind of sound, not an answer, but a tone that said *hurry*.

Eric reached around her to unhook her bra, dragged it slowly down until it fell to the floor, landing on his feet. He kicked it aside. "I know how hard your nipples get, what they feel like in my mouth." He ran his tongue around each nipple, enjoying the moan he drew from her. "I was the only man in that room to know all that about you, to know how perfectly you're put together. I was feeling pretty smug. And now I get to see all of you."

He finished undressing her, her body bathed in light from the hallway. "You're perfect." He dragged his fingers down her in feather-light touches. "And you're not saying a word. That's not like you at all."

"You said we should get this over with, but you keep *talking*."

The exasperation in her voice made him smile as he got rid of his own clothing. She sighed as she ran her hands over him, her fingers trembling, her breath uneven. She wrapped a hand around his erection. He sucked in a quick, hard breath and then grabbed her wrist, stopping her. "Not a good idea at the moment."

He slid a hand along her abdomen lower and lower, nestled his fingers, teasing.

"Also not a good idea at the moment," she said, moving his hand away. "It's going to be fast, and I want you inside."

They fell onto the bed, kissing, caressing, gripping, rolling. He ended up on top. Poised to enter her, he said, "Birth control?"

"It's okay. It's safe."

She was hot and slick and welcoming. And flattering in the way she climaxed instantly, clutching him, arching toward him, sounds of pleasure pouring from her. He couldn't have held back if he'd wanted to. She was everything he'd imagined in the fantasies that had awakened him at night and driven him crazy during the day. She'd been an obsession, a distraction, a goal. And now he was where he wanted to be, skin to skin, moving inside her, finding unimaginable pleasure in waves of sensation, knowing she was feeling the same.

When his world stopped spinning, he relaxed against her for a minute then rolled to his side with her, settling her in a comfortable position. She hadn't said anything. Hadn't even met his gaze. He ducked his head a little so that he could make eye contact.

"You okay?"

She nodded.

"Are you sure?"

"I've never been better in my entire life." Marcy was a little appalled at herself for telling him that, but the words had just spilled out.

"Well. That's good to hear," he said, sounding a little bewildered—or something. She wasn't sure.

She waited for him to say something equally flattering—or appalling—but he just brushed her hair with his fingers, moving it away from her face, then he slid his hand over her shoulder, down her back, over her rear. He lingered there. She closed her eyes, enjoying his touch.

"Do you have to rush off?" she asked as he dragged her leg over his hip and continued stroking then massaging her rear, his fingers sliding in and out, up and down, his palms kneading.

"Why would I?" he asked.

She moved closer to him, tucking her head below his chin. She loved the scent of him. "Um, what if Dylan's waiting up for you? He might get worried enough to call the police. He doesn't know where you are, does he?"

"I think it would take a lot more than being worried for Dylan to call the cops. And, no, I didn't tell him where I was going. *I* wasn't even sure where I was going. I tried to resist."

She drew in a long, slow breath as his caresses grew bolder.

"You're incredibly sensitive," he said. "Unbelievably sexy. You give your all to everything you do, don't you?"

"Why give less?" Although until now, she'd never realized she had so much to give. "Why did you try to resist?"

"You asked me to, citing reasons like how decrepit I am, and how different we are."

She smiled. "I didn't say you were decrepit. I said you were eleven years older than me, and that you've reached your goals, and I haven't yet. And we *are* different."

"Yes, we are."

She tipped her head back to look at him. "So why did you come to the bar?"

"Because your reasons for resisting would matter if I were proposing marriage, but I'm not. I'm proposing satisfying a need, a very powerful need. We have all the necessary things in common in order to do that."

He made perfect sense. So, why did it hurt to hear it? "This is something you expect to continue?"

"I'd like it to. Wouldn't you?"

She moved farther back. "You told me you're ready for marriage, ready for fatherhood."

"That's my goal."

"Which means you'll be on the lookout for a wife."

"That's pretty blunt, but at its core is truth."

"In the meantime, I'll do as a fill-in?"

"You'd rather be a one-night stand?"

"I—No. But…"

"But?"

Right then, Tom and Baby leaped onto the bed, purring. "Sorry," she said. "They usually sleep with me. I'll put them in the hall and shut the door."

When he didn't indicate she shouldn't, she got out of bed. After she shut the door, a light came on. He'd turned on a bedside lamp, and she was standing there, naked.

He wasn't looking at her, however, but the room. "What are we? Characters on an Arabian Nights movie set?"

She climbed into bed and pulled the sheet up as he gazed about the room. He was right. It was straight out of Arabian Nights, all red and gold and shimmering.

"Brutus is a little flamboyant," she said.

"That's like saying I know a little bit about math." He stretched out beside her, noticed she'd pulled the sheet up, but didn't cover up himself. "Where were we?"

You were wondering if I'd prefer to be a one-night stand. "I forget."

"No, you don't. It's an important question, Marcy. Do we keep going or is this it?"

"I don't know. I really don't."

"Okay, then, while you're making up your mind, how about we take a shower?"

Which they did, which led to a longer, much more leisurely, much more thorough lovemaking session. She sprawled, he cherished. He held her hair, she explored him. They gave, they took, they satisfied, they gratified. Finally sated, she curled up next to him and closed her eyes.

"I need to go," he said into her hair.

"Why?" she asked sleepily.

"Because it's 4:00 a.m., and I should be home when Dylan gets up."

She grabbed her robe from the bathroom door as he dressed. She didn't want to watch him. It gave the evening a finality she didn't want to think about.

When he was ready she opened the bedroom door. Tom and Baby sat there, yellow eyes glaring, tails swishing angrily.

"Will they attack?" Eric asked.

"They're annoyed, not violent." She stopped to pet each of them for a few seconds, and then they raced into her room and leaped onto the bed, making themselves at home. They would drape themselves over her as she slept. She wouldn't feel alone.

Hand in hand, Marcy and Eric walked downstairs and to the front door.

"Can you answer my question now?" he asked.

"No."

"So, now what?"

Now what? Now, I've gone and fallen in love with

you, which ruins everything. That's what. "Let's give it a couple of days, then we'll talk, okay?"

"Tell you what. You call me when you're ready." He pulled her close and kissed her. "It was one helluva night, Marcy."

She locked the door behind him, then inched the blinds apart in the living room window to watch him go. He gave her a little wave and took off.

Marcy climbed the stairs again, dropped her robe on the floor, turned off the lamp and climbed in bed, not taking the time or energy to pull on a night shirt. As soon as her head hit the pillows, the cats took their places, allowing her no exit.

She'd been awake for twenty-two hours. Important decisions should not be made without a good night's sleep. And the question would still be there when she woke up.

Chapter Twelve

"Two dozen?" Lori said. "Eric sent you two-dozen lavender roses?"

"They arrived just as I was leaving to come see you and the boys." Marcy was treating them to lunch at McDonald's. The kids were blowing off steam on the play equipment after eating, giving Marcy and Lori some time to talk.

"Are you sure he signed the card himself, not the florist?"

"I recognize his handwriting." Printed in a strong hand—THANK YOU FOR A NIGHT TO REMEMBER. ERIC.

Lori slid her straw in and out of the lid on her soda, almost making music. "So, he actually put a little effort into it. Have you looked up the meaning of lavender roses?"

"Never occurred to me." Marcy searched the internet on her phone, finding several slight variations on the meaning on different sites, but the primary one remained the same. "Love at first sight," she said out loud.

Lori lowered her cup to the table with a thud. "Really? Do you suppose he knows that?"

"I have no idea." She recalled their conversation about lust at first sight. Had he been referencing that discussion? Did he *mean* lust at first sight? Or love? Or neither? "Maybe he just liked the color and thought it suited me. Most people don't think about the meaning, do they?"

"I'm not the one to ask. The only time Doug gave me flowers was after Flynn was born. So, now what?"

"He left it up to me. If I want to continue, I have to contact *him*."

"Hm. And here we've been told forever that men like to do the pursuing, and we're supposed to play hard to get."

Marcy was more confused than ever. Sending her flowers was a lovely, romantic gesture, certainly nothing she'd expected. And he'd never seemed like a romantic to her, but he'd been proving her wrong.

"I can't think about it right now," Marcy said. "Tell me how your classes are going."

"One more semester and I'll be a full-fledged dental hygienist. It's so much easier this year with both boys in school all day."

"It's been a long, hard road for you." Marcy reached across the table and squeezed her friend's hand. "I'm so proud of you."

"I couldn't have done it without you, Marcy. Not just your unwavering friendship but the financial support.

If I ever track Doug down and get what he owes me, I'll pay you back."

"I've told you all along, it's a gift, not a loan. You can help someone else. Anyway, you've helped by being an example. I started college because of you. I'm sticking to the plan because of you. You're my hero."

"Thank you." Lori's voice shook a little. Doug had broken her self-confidence in so many ways.

Then in a flash of recognition, bright and clear, Marcy knew what her decision about Eric had to be.

Eric kept his cell phone in his pocket all day, even while tearing out dead shrubs and pruning plants that might be salvageable. He knew nothing about gardening, but Annie did, so she'd offered to be his consultant. An arborist would trim the trees. New sod had been ordered rather than trying to save the water-deprived lawns, front and back.

The work was hard, sweaty and satisfying.

Dylan groused about weeding and argued that his arm was healed enough for harder work, but Eric didn't want to take any chances. Next week they would demolish the kitchen in preparation for installing the new one. Dylan would be ready and could help.

Eric hadn't heard from Marcy. The florist verified that the roses had been delivered into her hands personally, but that was hours ago.

She'd been on his mind all day. Dylan had kidded him about sleeping in until nine, and there'd been a twinkle in his eyes, as if he knew where Eric had been and what time he'd come home. He wasn't going to give the kid any opportunities to bring it up.

What was she doing? Homework? She seemed diligent about her education, mostly getting A's, she'd told him once.

How late had she slept?

Did she like the flowers? He'd had a vision of her lying in bed with the petals strewn around and over her, the fragrance of the roses mingling with her own enticing scent.

If she invited him over again tonight, he would pick the petals off a few of the roses and scatter them over her... .

The sex last night had been phenomenal. Good the first time, extraordinary the second. He appreciated that she gave generously, but that she also accepted generously, as well.

Mutual satisfaction. The rarity of it made him appreciate it all the more—and want it again and again.

Why hadn't she called? Being in limbo was driving him crazy.

"Dude!"

Eric looked up at Dylan, who was holding out a tall glass of iced tea.

"Where you been? I called your name three times," Dylan said.

"Sorry." Eric took the glass. "I've been working out a problem. I have a tendency to go deep when I do that. Thanks." He lifted the glass a little then drank half of it.

"A math problem?" Dylan asked, sitting on the lawn. "I mean, I saw *Good Will Hunting*. I get that you math geniuses are always trying to figure out stuff."

Well, Marcy was a hot little number, but he couldn't exactly tell Dylan that. "Contrary to common stereotyping, math experts, genius or otherwise, aren't always thinking about theorems."

"What's a theorem?"

"A statement that has been proven based on previously established statements."

"Like I'm never going to have a girlfriend because no one's ever said yes when I asked them out?"

Eric totally identified—and was sympathetic. "Girls say no for a lot of reasons. In my case, because I was a nerd for a long time. I didn't know how to relate to girls, only to numbers. But I got better at it in college, and I did okay. Then my parents died and I had four siblings to raise. I took that responsibility seriously, and most girls didn't want to get involved."

"Sort of like guys not wanting to date single moms."

"Or the opposite. Women not wanting to date single dads."

"That happens?"

"Technically, that's what I was, except they were all teenagers with big issues of their own. Instead of being little brats, they were big ones." He grinned. "But they all came out okay in the end, and we're great friends now."

Dylan thought about that. "I guess you're right. Different situation but same results."

"So, how many girls have turned you down?"

"Two."

Even though Dylan said it in such a discouraged tone, Eric laughed. He couldn't help it. "I'm sure two doesn't qualify as a rejection theorem. Remember what Marcy said? You have hair girls want to touch, and a great smile. It's the communication skills—which I think are improving—that have held you back. I bet if you asked now, you'd get a different response. I've been turned down plenty, and I haven't given up."

His phone rang. Marcy. "I'll be back," he said to Dylan, then walked toward the house as he said hello.

"Thank you for the roses," she said. "They're beautiful."

So are you. "I'm glad you like them." He paused, letting her guide the conversation. He'd just reached the kitchen, gaining privacy. She could talk sexy if she wanted. And he could respond.

"Last night was wonderful," she said.

"I thought so, too."

"But it can't happen again, Eric."

He sat in the nearest chair. He hadn't expected that. "Why? The age thing?"

"Only as it relates to you being where you are in your life now, as opposed to where I am in mine. I need to finish college and get a career going. I've told you that. It's more than just important to me. It's critical."

"How does our sleeping together cancel that out for you?"

"Contrary to the impression you must have of me, I don't sleep around, Eric. I've had relationships, and they've mattered. I haven't slept with someone I haven't cared about. You told me you're looking for someone permanent. Even if you were interested in me in that way, I'm not ready. And you can't wait. We had a case of lust at first sight, and we acted on it. I don't regret that for one second. It was something we needed to do, and we did it."

He didn't want her to walk out of his life—or Dylan's. "I'd like to stay friends. Dylan needs you."

She didn't answer right away, and when she did it sounded as if she was crying—or trying hard not to.

"I won't abandon him," she said. "He's had enough of that in his life."

Eric closed his eyes for a few seconds. "By default that means you'll have to see me, too. Can you deal with that?"

"Sure."

Sure. As if it was no big deal.

"In fact, tell him I'll pick him up Tuesday morning for an interview with Julia. Does he have something business casual to wear?"

"I'll make sure he does. But he can take the bus. He can catch one on campus. You can meet him at a stop in Sacramento. There's no reason for you to drive here and back twice."

"I don't mind. I—"

"He needs to do this, Marcy. I'll figure where he can meet you and text you the information. Thanks for calling." He hung up, not waiting for her to say goodbye or whatever else she might have to say, then he went upstairs and into his bedroom. He shut the door and sat in the window seat overlooking the front yard. Annie and Lucy were playing with a ball next door. Kids were riding bicycles and skateboards. Life went on as normal.

Except for him. Marcy's rejection had staggered him. He hadn't expected it—either the rejection or his reaction. He didn't know what to make of it, couldn't interpret her tone of voice because he'd been so focused on the words themselves, how they'd shouted in his head, shouting so loudly they'd drowned out the question that had been echoing there much of the time today.

He pulled out his cell and dialed her.

"Hello?" She said the word hesitantly.

"When I asked you last night about birth control, you said it was safe. What did you mean? Are you on the pill?"

"No. The timing's off, that's all. It's not my fertile time of month."

"Are you sure?"

"I'm sure."

He rubbed his forehead. "If it turns out that you're pregnant, you'll tell me."

"Of course I would, but I won't be, Eric."

"Okay. Thanks." Again he hung up without saying goodbye or waiting for her to.

He shoved his phone in his pocket and went outside to join Dylan, a fellow member of the rejection club. He'd reached the deck when his phone rang, but it was his sister, not Marcy.

"Hey, Becca."

"Hi yourself. How's everything going? You never write. You never call."

"Busy. How're you?"

"Busy, too. But I've been thinking we need to have double housewarming parties. Kincaid will be finishing up our place next week, then I hear he's coming to do your kitchen the following week. I called the brothers. They could fly in the next weekend. We can have a party at our place on Saturday then yours on Sunday, then you can take them to the airport that night. Work for you?"

It was just what he needed—a distraction and a deadline. "I'm glad you thought of it. May I bring my roommate?"

"Your room— Oh, Dylan! Sure. Marcy, too, of course."

"I don't think so, but thanks."

She knew him well enough not to push. "How about your neighbor I've been hearing about. Annie?"

"No, thanks."

"Well, feel free to invite someone, if you feel like it. Gavin insisted on having a huge dining room. We can comfortably seat twelve."

"I'll think about it."

"Are you okay, Eric?"

"I will be in a few weeks, when life has settled down."

"Is it hard having Dylan around?"

"No. In fact, I'm glad it worked out the way it did." He had someone to think about other than himself. Someone who needed him. "I'll firm up flight plans with the brothers. Thanks again, Bec." One of the reasons he'd chosen this area was so that he could see his sister more often, and she was making that happen. "I'll talk to you soon."

Eric ended the call and tucked the phone away.

"Everything okay?" Dylan asked.

Eric told him about the two housewarming parties a few weekends from now.

"I had a foster brother for a few years, but we didn't keep in touch," Dylan said. "I guess it's a fantasy of only kids to want the big, loud family. And for me, having parents who were kinda old meant things were quieter, too, I guess. They were over fifty when they took me in."

If Eric didn't hurry up and find the right woman to marry and start having children, he'd be the age of

Dylan's parents—and his kids would think he was old. "I guess there are pros and cons to both situations."

"What happened to your parents?" Dylan asked.

"A car accident on an icy road late at night." His mother had needed to interview a prisoner. His father hadn't wanted her driving alone in the weather, so he'd gone with her.

If she hadn't been working. If she hadn't had a profession that took her away from home at all hours...

His resentment over his mother's choice to work instead of being home with her family had escalated through the years instead of declining. Their lives would've turned out so differently, if only...

He didn't understand Marcy's need for a career, either, especially since she'd chosen a field that didn't even seem to suit her. On the other hand, he admired Annie's decision to stay home with Lucy as long as she could afford to.

"You're zoning again," Dylan said.

"Sorry. I was remembering."

Dylan nodded. "Where will your brothers stay when they come?"

"At a hotel. I'll check out what's available in Davis. They usually stay in Sacramento."

"How about the housewarming party? What happens at one?"

Eric gave it some thought. "Food and drink, I guess. People bring presents like house plants."

"People, like who? Neighbors? People you work with?"

Eric scratched his head. "I don't have a clue. I suppose it could be anyone."

"I'll bet Marcy knows."

Last night was wonderful, but it can't happen again, she'd said. "Maybe." He glanced toward the fence. "Annie probably does, too."

"Don't ask her. Please."

"Why not?"

"She's already got her hopes up. Unless you want more with her? Maybe you do." Dylan didn't look up but continued to tug weeds.

Eric wasn't going to get into a discussion of such things with the boy. "I can hire a caterer."

"Or Marcy. She's a good cook."

Or Marcy. He would think about it. "Speaking of Marcy, she said she would take you to At Your Service on Tuesday." They discussed Dylan taking the bus and what to wear. Eric steered the discussion away from Marcy. He needed time to absorb her rejection and come up with a new plan. She seemed determined to follow her path for now. He didn't think anything he said would change her mind.

But as for seeing her again—a necessity if he asked her to help with the party—he wasn't sure he was ready for that, even though he'd been the one to say let's be friends.

All he knew for sure was that last night ranked number one on his list of memories. He wouldn't stop picturing her in bed anytime soon—which really put a monkey wrench into his plans to find a wife and start a family.

So much for fresh beginnings.

At least the loss of Jamie had found a comfortable place in his heart. He would remember his "little brother" fondly and forever, but it no longer hurt. He gave credit to Marcy for that.

And Dylan.

He glanced at the teenager as he dug in the earth, wondering what would've become of him had he not broken into the house?

Eric's new life hadn't turned out to be anywhere near what he'd expected when he'd made the move to California.

Time would tell if that was a good thing.

Chapter Thirteen

Nerves had Marcy tapping her fingers on her steering wheel, even without music playing. She hadn't seen Eric since they'd slept together nine days ago, and now she was driving to his house to discuss a job because he refused to give her the details over the phone. Otherwise they'd spoken only once—to arrange Dylan's bus trip to Sacramento last week.

Dylan called her daily, but he hadn't dropped any hints about what Eric wanted. Either Dylan didn't know or he was keeping quiet about it. He'd done well at his interview with Julia Swanson, but no temp jobs had come along for him yet. Nor had his job hunting in Davis resulted in any offers.

Marcy turned onto Eric's street and noticed portable barriers along the sidewalks and the street itself clear of cars. She pulled into Eric's driveway. Dylan rushed from the backyard to the driveway.

"You're just in time," he said. "They're closing the street in five minutes."

"For what?"

"A block party. They have it every Labor Day."

She turned off the engine. "You mean I won't be able to leave?"

"I don't know. Are those the dogs?"

She'd brought the dogs included in her latest house-sitting job, thinking they would only be gone for a couple of hours. Both were yelping and digging in their carriers. They were extremely high-energy and needed constant attention or they became destructive.

"Yes, they're—"

Eric came up behind Dylan. Everything inside her clenched, then melted. She'd thought she remembered him perfectly, but he was even more handsome than she recalled, his eyes a darker brown, his hair softer, his body harder.

His smile, however, was hesitant. "Hi, Marcy."

"Hi."

"Can I shut the gate so we can let the dogs out?" Dylan asked.

Eric nodded. He bent lower to look into the back seat. "Jack Russell terriers?" he asked.

"Frasier and Niles," Marcy said, drawing a smile from Eric. "Their owners are both psychiatrists."

He laughed. "Figures. They must be a handful."

"An understatement, although they're really smart and well trained." She climbed out, then opened the back door as Dylan loped back. He lifted the carriers out and opened them. They were off and running, checking out everything in sight at warp speed. Dylan went after them, laughing as they all chased each other.

"You look good," he said, eyeing her thoughtfully, his expression warm.

"Thanks." She didn't want to be drawn toward him. She'd thought enough time had passed. Obviously it hadn't, because she wanted to grab his hand, take him upstairs and spend the next twenty-four hours in bed with him, making love, holding him, being held. Talking. She'd missed their nighttime talks in the chairs by the fireplace.

"Dylan said there's a block party going on?" she asked. "Does that mean I can't get out?"

"You can drive a couple of blocks over, park and walk back—if they haven't put up the barriers. Apparently people bring out tables and chairs into the street for a big picnic. They set up games for the kids. It lasts until nine o'clock."

She crossed her arms. "And you didn't think to mention this on the phone because?"

"I didn't know until ten minutes ago that the street would be blocked off. I knew there was a party, but that's all."

She wondered if that was true. "So now I'm stuck here for five hours."

"Let me go take a look. Be right back." He jogged up the driveway, slipped out the gate. When he reached the sidewalk he looked both directions then came back. "The corners are blocked off and people have already moved tables and chairs into the street. Sorry."

He didn't sound sorry, not one bit, but there was nothing she could do about it. "I'll need a bowl for water for the dogs."

"No problem. Dylan! We're going inside."

"Okay!"

They headed into the kitchen. Marcy came to a stop inside the door. "There's no kitchen."

"There's a refrigerator and a microwave. Who needs more than that?"

He'd stopped close behind her. His hand came to rest at the small of her back. She wanted to move but she didn't—couldn't. She closed her eyes instead and just enjoyed the sensation.

"On Thursday, when summer session ends, we'll start on the new kitchen. We hope to be done by the time fall semester starts eleven days later." He moved around her, his hand dragging along her back then her arm before losing contact. Out of a big cardboard box he dug out a bowl and headed for the hall half-bath. "Be right back," he said, taking the full bowl outside.

Marcy sat at the kitchen table and watched him put the bowl on the deck then walk down the stairs to say something to Dylan, who nodded and continued to play with the dogs. Moments later, Eric sat next to Marcy at the table, where they both could watch Dylan and the dogs.

"You two seem to be getting along well," Marcy said.

"We're doing okay."

It was a generic statement that didn't tell her much, but he seemed a little stiff. Why? Because she wanted to rub his back, she clasped her hands in her lap. "What's the job you want to talk about?"

He shifted to face her. "It would be for the last Sunday of the month. My brothers are coming in for the weekend. Becca's having a housewarming party on Saturday that same weekend in Chance City now that Kincaid has finished their renovations. She decided I should have one on Sunday before my brothers have to fly out. I'd like you to do all the planning, make sure it goes okay. I don't know which caterer to contact. I imagine you do."

She didn't want to spend more time with his terrific sister or meet his brothers, and yet she didn't want to let just anyone put together the party for him, either. Her protectiveness toward him gave her pause, but not for long. "How many people?"

He seemed to relax—at least his back wasn't as stiff. "The brothers. Becca and Gavin. Shana. Kincaid. Dylan. A couple of people from work."

"Annie?"

"No. I'll do something for the neighbors later, I think."

Marcy ignored the relief she felt about him not wanting to include Annie. She reached for her purse and the pad of paper she always carried. "Do you want a sit-down dinner? Barbecue? Buffet?"

"What do you think?"

"The weather could still be a hundred by then or eighty. Maybe we could do a barbecue and buffet. You could use the dining room if it's too hot outside."

"Whatever you think is best. Um, I'd appreciate it if you could come over when the kitchen is finished and help me set it up, see what other items I need. Could you do that?"

"I guess so. If you don't mind, I'd rather do the food for the party than have it catered. You could barbecue. I'd do the rest." Which would feel dangerously like they were a couple, she knew. "It's the kind of event I love to do and don't get to very often."

"I'll sign off on whatever you want. Marcy," he said, making eye contact. "Thank you. For everything before, and for this."

Her throat convulsed a little, trapping words. She nodded. Would she ever get over him? Ever stop wanting him? It wasn't supposed to be this way. She'd slept with him. She should be able to move on.

"How're your classes going?"

She swallowed. "Good. I'm looking forward to moving on to Sac State and wrapping it all up. It's my goal to finish in two years. It took me four years to get this far. I've been saving like crazy. I'll house-sit those final four semesters but I won't take any other jobs. College will be my job."

Dylan rushed in. "Did you bring leashes? I could walk the dogs around the block."

"In the trunk of my car," she said. "They're kid-friendly and other-dog-friendly, but they both hate cats, so be careful."

"I'll walk them up to Jason's. He's a new friend on the block," Dylan added. "Don't expect me back for half an hour, maybe longer. If that's okay, Marcy?"

"Jason has a hot sister," Eric said to her.

"Ah," she said, understanding. "Sure, that's fine."

Dylan grinned then he was off.

Quiet settled between Marcy and Eric. Street noise filtered into the room through open windows, the sound of people calling out to each other, and children's laughter.

"Do you have particular duties for this shindig?" she asked.

"I'm the new kid on the block, and one without a kitchen, at that. I was told specifically not to bring anything." Eric reached under the table, curved his hand over both of hers clenched in her lap. He had no doubt that Dylan had left to give them time alone. He didn't know if his attention would be welcomed by Marcy, but he needed to try. Every day that passed he wanted her more. "I've missed you."

She didn't say anything, didn't look at him, but he knew her well enough to know she was feeling the same things he was.

"There's something upstairs I want to show you," he said.

"Your etchings?" she asked, her eyes finally taking on some sparkle.

"I guess you could call them designs, of a sort."

"What sort?"

"Designs on you."

"We decided this shouldn't go any further."

"You decided. I'm hoping to change your mind." He leaned close and kissed her. He felt her need when he touched his lips to hers—or maybe that was just coming from his own body. She didn't try to stop him.

"I want you, Marcy." *Like nothing else in the world, ever.*

"What if Dylan comes back early?" Her voice was tight and barely audible.

"He won't."

"How can you be sure? He—"

"Marcy, I promise you, he won't."

"What, some secret code passed between you before he left?"

"He's very intuitive. And we're wasting time." He

stood, keeping hold of her hands and urging her along with him, but it wasn't long before she lunged at him and kissed him hard and with a need that matched his.

"Hurry," she said.

They raced up the stairs and into his room, stripped off each other's clothes and landed on the bed, entwined and kissing, mutual sounds of pleasure filling the room.

"We'll need birth control," she said.

"Done." He got what he needed from his night stand. "Where were we?"

"I want to be on top this time," she whispered.

"You think I'd refuse that?" he asked, stretching out, helping her to straddle him.

He was sure he would never forget the glorious sight of her, her hair curling wildly around her, her breasts swaying, her nipples hard as she offered herself freely, openly. He helped her maneuver herself so that she could take him inside, then they both closed their eyes and lay still, enjoying the connection, the ecstasy.

"You are exquisite," he said, caressing her breasts, angling up to taste and savor her.

He gripped her thighs as she straightened and then began to move, grabbing the headboard to keep herself steady. He loved watching her, loved seeing the look of rapture on her face.

He watched her find satisfaction, waited for her to stop moving, then maneuvered her onto her back, wanting the sweet fullness of her body under him. He took it slow, dragged it out, smiled when she said, "Oh! Again," as if caught off guard, then he found home with her, and deep pleasure, followed by a surprising peace. Sweat adhered them. Their breaths were shaky and shallow.

"We can't linger," she said, tucking herself close as they rolled to their sides, steam rising between them.

"I know." He stroked her hair, ran a hand down her body, kissed her. He couldn't get enough of her. He wondered what it all meant. Did this change her mind? "Marcy—"

"Shh." She put a finger against his lips. "Let's not talk about it. Not yet." She shoved herself off the bed and hurried into his bathroom, scooping up her clothes as she went. He gathered his own and went into the guest bath to clean up. They met on the landing in a few minutes.

She went up on tiptoe and kissed him, framing his face with her hands. It seemed to him like the most loving gesture anyone had ever made.

"Let's go back to the kitchen and plan the party," she said. "I want Dylan to find us there."

They'd just reached the bottom of the stairs when someone knocked. It was Annie, with Lucy.

Marcy's face heated. She made sure there was distance between her and Eric, but she had a feeling Annie would see the truth.

Annie smiled, offered an overly cheerful greeting, then turned her attention on Eric. "The party's started."

"Thanks. We'll be out there soon."

"Good. How are you, Marcy?"

"I'm well, thank you. And you?"

"I'm excellent, thank you for asking. Everything's looking bright."

"How nice for you." Marcy was proud of how she kept sarcasm out of her voice.

Annie left. Eric shut the door behind her, then silence

descended between him and Marcy. She struggled for something to say.

"Shall we start planning?" she asked finally.

"There's nothing between us, Marcy. Annie and me."

"Have you told her that?"

He frowned. "Do I have to spell it out for her?"

"In a kind way, yes, I think you do. She's…hopeful. You apparently haven't discouraged her."

"I've never asked her out. Never touched her." He leaned close. "I think you're misreading her. She doesn't come on to me at all. Look, she's the kind of woman I used to go for, but not anymore."

"Why's that?"

"She never disagrees with me. She doesn't have opinions of her own. Frankly, she's boring. And she's needy."

He set his hands on Marcy's shoulders and guided her toward the kitchen. The moment they sat, Dylan came through the back door. He gave them both a look of curiosity.

"The dogs are worn out," he said. "They both went into their carriers and fell asleep. I put them in the shade."

"Thanks," Marcy said. "Did they help you score points with Hot Sister?"

He grinned. "Major." He got a soda out of the refrigerator. "Want one?"

Cold drinks were handed out, then Dylan sat at the table with them, like so many times before, almost as if she'd never left.

"Are you going to help Eric with the party?" he asked.

"I am. I think it'll be fun." And maybe a little difficult, meeting the rest of his family, she thought. "It sounds like you've settled in here."

"I don't take it for granted," he said right away with a glance at Eric.

"He's worked hard."

The doorbell rang three times. "That's Jason," Dylan said, hopping up. "He said he'd come get me when he was going to the party."

"If Hot Sister is with him, I'd like to meet her," Marcy said.

"She has a boyfriend." He hurried out.

"Well, that's disappointing," Marcy said.

"The guy is a jerk, according to Dylan, so he figures he has a chance."

"I guess no one's told him that girls, especially teenage girls, are drawn to bad boys."

Eric took her hand in his and held it. "Are you?"

"Not now. But when I was sixteen? You bet. His name was Speck."

Eric's brows went up. "Your first?"

She shook her head. He was brushing her hand with his thumb, keeping her in a constant state of arousal. Did he know that? "My first didn't happen until I was twenty. Late bloomer."

"Me, too. I was also twenty."

"Really? What was her name?"

"Stella. Stella Bella, in fact."

"Seriously?"

"Cross my heart. She was the T.A. for one of my calculus professors. She was thirty. I thought I'd died and gone to heaven. How about you?"

Marcy was surprised they were having this discussion, but also glad. Anything to take the focus off of her and their relationship. "I fancied myself in love, so although it was mostly a lot of fumbling around, I wasn't really disappointed. He didn't stay around long, which broke my heart."

"Stella didn't, either, which didn't break my heart, however. I always kind of appreciated her for showing me the ropes." He grinned.

"As did the women who followed, I imagine."

"I never asked." His eyes twinkled. He leaned back a little. "I tell you things I've never told anyone. I've gotten closer to you faster than to anyone else. It's as if when I met you, I already knew you."

"We did talk for days on the phone while you traveled."

He hesitated then shrugged. "That was probably part of it."

Was he trying to say she was his soul mate? It was a term she understood in theory but had never experienced. She decided to change the subject and grabbed her pad and pen. They discussed party plans for a while, and then Eric said, "We should probably make an appearance."

"You go ahead and mingle. I've got my laptop. I'm just going to stay here and do some work."

He cocked his head. "Sometimes you really surprise me."

"In what way?"

"You're very direct about most things, yet you won't let my neighbors see you with me."

She shrugged.

"Because they will make assumptions?" he asked.

"Yes." And she might not do a good job of hiding her feelings, either. She couldn't even tell him that what had just happened upstairs in his bedroom was a mistake, because it wasn't. It'd happened because need had trumped caution once again.

And she loved him.

How could that be a mistake? Bad timing, maybe. But when someone loved, it showed. So she would stay inside and avoid controversy.

"I'll come back in a little while," he said.

"I'll be here." She smiled, as if making a joke out of the fact she couldn't leave anyway.

Hours later, the street was opened to traffic again. Dylan and Jason had long ago settled into playing video games in the living room, with Eric overseeing and occasionally competing. The dogs loved the action and noise, moving from boy to boy for scratching and petting. Marcy had curled up in a chair with her laptop.

It could be like this. Kids and activity and the man she loved. She could have it all.

Except that Eric wasn't in love with her. He only wanted a physical relationship—he'd even said so. And she had her own goals to attain.

She closed her eyes for a few seconds, trying to find equilibrium. When had her life gotten so complicated, she wondered.

The current video game ended with Dylan the victor. Time for Marcy to make her move.

"Eric, can you take a look at this? I've put a plan together. And Dylan, would you put the dogs in their carriers, please? Maybe they should be let out in the backyard first."

"Sure," Dylan said. He and Jason took the dogs out while Eric crouched beside her.

She went down the list of food and drink she'd decided on. "When I come help you put your kitchen in order, I'll know what you'll need otherwise."

"Feel free to drop by while we're working. See the progress."

"That week I'll be working in downtown Sacramento as a receptionist, Monday through Friday, plus I have another house-sitting job. No free time."

"How about an evening this week? If I come to you?" he asked, lowering his voice.

"Okay," she whispered. "One night."

"Thursday? We could go out to dinner."

She nodded then stood, annoyed at herself for not having the willpower to tell him no, sure that she would get hurt and yet unable to stop it from happening.

He rested his hand at the base of her spine as they walked to the kitchen door. Such a small touch to garner such a big reaction. She sucked in her breath as he cupped her rear, then patted it lightly, playfully, as she opened the back door. She'd wanted a relationship like this forever. Had ached for a man who couldn't keep his hands off her, who valued her opinions, who was responsible and fun.

She'd met a lot of men who were fun, but a lot fewer who were responsible.

She gave Dylan a hug goodbye, then after a slight hesitation, hugged Eric as well. The dogs were making a lot of noise as she got into the car. It was nine-thirty at night, and the temperature was perfect. She rolled down her window and waved goodbye.

Dylan and Eric stood in the driveway watching her go. She felt as if she were abandoning them.

A sense of loss jabbed at her. She should be there,

with them. They had become her family. She shouldn't be driving away.

But she continued on to the freeway. The dogs settled down.

And on Thursday she would see him again, feel his arms around her, hear him compliment and appreciate her.

It wasn't where she'd expected to be at this point in her life, and there was probably a price she would have to pay for it, too.

Time would tell.

Chapter Fourteen

Eric and Marcy lay in bed Thursday evening, naked and sated, talking lazily. "Is it easy or hard for you," he asked, "living in a different house all the time?"

"I don't take on a brand-new client very often any-more, so there's a certain familiarity with almost every house for me. First times are more problematic. I do like houses with alarms. I sleep better. But the houses I watch are mostly in very good neighborhoods."

She was on her side, one leg draped over his, her hand resting against his chest. Her voice was low and relaxed, as if she could drop off to sleep anytime, even though it was only eight-thirty. He felt her breath, warm and steady, on his neck as she spoke.

"What was your most interesting assignment?"

She laughed softly. "A two-week job for Elmer Wain-wright."

"The software mogul? He lives in Sacramento?"

"San Francisco. He got my name from a friend of a friend. The man never slows down, never sits down. I don't think he sleeps, even. And his whole house is run electronically. There's a three-inch binder with instructions. I locked myself in and couldn't get out."

He laughed. "I'm sorry. I know it's not funny, but—"

"Oh, it's hysterical. Now. A different kind of hysterical then. It took me two days to figure out how to open the front door."

"Why didn't you call him?"

"I didn't want him to think I was an idiot."

Eric smiled at the ceiling. He threaded her hair with his fingers. It was the most relaxed they'd been with each other. Not that the sex hadn't been powerful and satisfying, but the aftermath was different this time.

"You said you were offered your job back as a flight attendant, but you didn't want to move back east. Why?"

"My friend Lori needed me. Her husband walked out when their boys were four and two. He emptied the bank accounts and left her without anything. We've been best friends since we were kids. I couldn't abandon her."

"Do you help support her?"

After a slight hesitation, she nodded. "She would've done the same for me."

"So, the money you save by not having a place to live goes to her?"

"Some of it. In return I always—almost always—have a place to stay."

He could tell she didn't really want to talk about it, but they'd become very open with each other, asking questions that might normally seem too personal this early in a relationship.

"Do you have a best friend?" she asked.

"I guess my brothers fit that title, Sam most of all. He's two years younger. Trent and Jeff are close, as well."

"Where does Becca fit in?"

"We share her." He smiled at the thought. "She's the youngest. We all worried about her, protected her, even though she balked at our care, and pretty much did what she wanted, anyway. She chose well with Gavin. They make a good team."

"Do you think marriage should be teamwork?" she asked.

"In the sense that you're striving toward the same goals, yes. And that you work together to achieve them."

She rested her chin on his chest and smiled at him. "Did you play football?"

"Yes."

"I'll bet you were the quarterback."

"You'd win that bet." He ran a hand down her spine, pressing lightly, drawing moans. "Roll onto your stomach."

She did, and he straddled her to give her a massage, taking his time, eventually turning it into a sensual experience, arousing her, not letting her find satisfaction until he was ready to let her.

"My turn," she said, shoving him onto his stomach. She'd just begun running her fingernails down his back when his cell phone rang. "It's Dylan," she said when she passed the phone to him.

"What's up, Dylan?" Eric asked.

"My dad's here."

"What?"

"He's in your living room. Can you come home?"

"I'm on my way." He ended the call. "His dad tracked him down. He's at the house."

"I want to go, too," Marcy said as he grabbed his jeans.

He laid a hand on her arm. "You can't. You know that. Dylan would realize we've been together."

She frowned, and then pulled on her robe instead of her clothes. "So much for teamwork."

He finished dressing then went up to her. "This is probably going to sound cold, but we've been honest with each other all along, and we need to stay honest." He took her hands in his. "I know you have a vested interest in Dylan, but he's my responsibility. We're not married, Marcy. There's no teamwork involved here."

She tossed her head a little. "I know that. You'll call me, though, right?"

"Yes." He kissed her. "I'm sorry our evening was cut short."

She took his face in her hands and turned the kiss into something beyond a quick good-night. "Don't forget I owe you one."

His laugh came out in an appreciative burst. "Like I'd forget that."

On the drive home, Eric stopped thinking about Marcy and thought ahead to Dylan. He sounded scared. Or maybe just panicked. If he'd been scared he probably wouldn't have let his dad in the house.

Eric didn't bother parking in the driveway, but pulled up behind an older-model sedan. Dylan opened the front door when Eric reached it.

"Are you okay?" he asked the boy, who nodded.

A man stood. Dylan had said his father was sixty-five, but he looked older. He was small and wiry, a little stooped. He clenched a Sacramento River Cats ball cap in his hands. He held out a hand to Eric. "I'm John Dunning. Dylan's my boy."

"Eric Sheridan," he said. "Please, have a seat. Have you been talking?" he asked Dylan.

"I've been trying to," John said. "Dylan's not of a mind to converse with me, I guess."

"How did you locate him?"

"He called an old friend, who called me. I've been looking for him for months. The friend knew I was worried." He looked at Dylan. "I know it was wrong to throw you out, son. I was hurtin'. That's all I can say about that. You weren't being exactly easy to have around, either."

"Because *I* was hurting." Dylan thumped his chest. "I lost someone special, too."

"I'm sorry. I really am."

For a moment neither of them spoke again.

"What did you come here to say to Dylan?" Eric asked.

John twisted his cap in his hands. "That he's welcome to come home."

For all that Eric had been guiding Dylan toward independence, Eric realized with sudden clarity that he didn't want the boy to go. Eric could give him chances his dad couldn't.

It wasn't his decision, however.

After a long silence, Dylan looked at Eric. "Do I have to make up mind right now?"

"No." Eric faced John. "I figure you want what's best for him, so he should take his time deciding, right?"

The man nodded. "Your mom's been haunting me,"

he said to Dylan. "I did wrong by you. But you seem to have done okay. I worried for nothing."

"Nothing?" Dylan exploded, jumping up, shoving his hands through his hair, then stretching his arms open wide. "I was living on the streets for three months. I didn't know where my next meal would come from or where I would sleep. I endured...horrible things. Threats. Violence. The pain of knowing you didn't love me even after twelve years of living with you, being like your son, even though you never adopted me. I can't forgive you."

He raced up the stairs, slammed his bedroom door behind him. The ensuing quiet hung heavy.

"I didn't know," John said, shock and confusion in his eyes.

"You should have." It was a harsh thing to say, but it needed saying, Eric decided. "Maybe he will forgive you someday, but don't think he'll forget soon. It changed him. I think you'll find him a different young man now."

"How did you get involved?"

"I had just moved in here, and he came looking for work." Eric figured Marcy would be proud of him for the lie. Dylan could choose to tell his dad the truth if he wanted. "When I found out he was homeless, I gave him a room. He's worked hard, and he's thrived."

John nodded then stood. "Well, he knows my number."

"May I have it, as well?"

They exchanged phone numbers then Eric walked him to his car. "Give him time. He has deep roots with you and his mom."

"Thank you." He stuck out his hand. "For everything you've done."

"It was my pleasure."

Eric watched him drive off, and then he parked his car in the garage. By the time he'd gotten inside, Dylan was sitting in a chair in the living room.

"I'm sorry I had to call," he said.

"It's fine." Eric sat down opposite him. "Are you okay?"

He shrugged. "Kinda caught me off guard, him just showing up."

"What do you want to do?"

He looked around, at nothing, at everything, then he blew out a long breath. "Is it so wrong that I want to stay with you?"

He knew that Dylan saw Eric as his rescuer, that his attachment was strong. "I understand why you feel that way. You also have a twelve-year history with your dad."

"But—"

Eric leaned forward. "But the goal all along has been for you to be independent. That hasn't changed. Don't try to figure it out tonight. Give it at least until we're done with the kitchen renovation. Maybe give your dad a call now and then and see what comes of it."

"Yeah. Okay. Thanks." He shifted in his chair a little. "So, I guess Marcy wasn't too happy that you wouldn't let her come with you, huh?"

Eric said nothing.

"Come on, dude. You think I don't know? You're nuts about each other. So, she was mad, wasn't she?"

"Irritated," Eric said, giving in. "She's your biggest fan."

"My mom would've loved her. They're not alike except that they're good mother types. Television-mother types."

Eric smiled. He agreed. "Are you ready to start building a kitchen tomorrow?" Eric asked, changing the subject.

"Ready."

"Me, too." Eric needed the physical labor, anything to clear his mind, or more precisely, it would be a way for Marcy not to be taking up so much space there. Things were starting to get more serious between them, and they both knew they weren't destined for the long term. They were too different, had vastly different goals. Were in different stages in their lives, as Marcy constantly reminded him.

"I'm going to bed," Dylan said. He stood and headed to the stairs. "When you call Marcy, tell her I said hi."

Eric just gave him the look, and he laughed.

Marcy answered on the first ring. "What happened?"

"First of all, Dylan says to say hi."

"Tell him hi back. What *happened?*"

He filled her in, could sense her tension lessening as he laid it out for her.

"He can't force Dylan to go home, can he?" she said. "He's eighteen."

"No, he can't force him, but I think his dad might be prepared to help him with his education, whether it's college or a training school to become a mechanic. We need to stay out of his decision, Marcy."

"I know you're right. It's just hard. I've already come to love him like a little brother."

Eric knew that feeling very well. "Yes."

They talked a little longer then said good-night. He

probably wouldn't see her until a week from Sunday, when the kitchen should be done and she would help set it up. Nine days.

At the moment, it seemed an eternity, especially because he'd left with her promise of owing him one.

Maybe he could find a couple of hours during the week, after all.

He smiled, liking the goal, even though he knew it would be just about impossible to achieve.

Chapter Fifteen

Marcy was exhausted—or tuckered out, as her mom would say. It'd been a long week of working in an office all day plus house-sitting, which included walking a Great Dane named George twice a day, a feat that eliminated the need for any other exercise. She'd had two papers due at the same time, and her usual Friday and Saturday night job at Score.

It was four o'clock on Sunday. She'd slept late, walked the dog, then waited eagerly for the homeowner to return. Now she was pulling into Eric's driveway to see the new kitchen and finalize plans for the party.

Between her three jobs, she'd earned a lot of money for one week, but as she climbed out of her car, stretching and yawning, she wondered if it'd been worth it. She couldn't catch up this week, either. She had a three-day job midweek but no house-sitting, which also meant she would be at Lori's with two rambunctious kids who adored her and wanted her constant attention. Plus nights spent sleeping on a very old, uncomfortable couch.

"Just one full night's sleep," she muttered. "Twelve hours. That ought to do it."

"Twelve hours ought to do what?" Eric asked, coming up from behind her as she yawned again.

"Sleep," she said, patting her mouth and smiling. He looked wonderful. They'd talked on the phone a few times during the week but hadn't managed to find any spare moments to see each other. Right now she could easily fall into his arms and let him take care of her. She could even picture him tucking her in bed and kissing her good-night. She crossed her arms instead, preventing either of them from even instigating a hug.

"You do look a little pale," he said, keeping his distance, apparently picking up on her cue. "Are you sure it's just lack of sleep? You're not coming down with something?"

"I don't have time to come down with something." She smiled at him. "I can't wait to see the kitchen."

"Let's go through the front door." They walked up the driveway.

"Is Dylan home?"

"He and Jason took off on their bikes a while ago. He knew what time you were coming, so I expect he'll be along soon."

"Should I wait until he gets back? I know he was a big part of the process."

"That's very thoughtful of you. He was more than just a big part, Marcy. He did major work. The kid knows how to handle power tools. He puts his head down and works. Even Kincaid commented on it, and he's apparently the man who never slows down, never does anything less than stellar work. Yes, I think Dylan's proud of the kitchen."

"And you?"

"Very happy with how it turned out, and I learned a whole lot. Like it's better to hire experts." He grinned. "I liked being part of the process, but I won't tackle re-doing the bathrooms on my own."

They went inside the house, took seats in their usual living-room chairs. She wished she could just curl up in his lap, to sleep and to be held. She'd missed him a whole lot.

"How are things going with his dad?" she asked.

"*Tentatively* is a good word, I think. Dylan's torn about it all." He cocked his head. "If you need a nap, feel free to use my bed."

"I'll be okay, thanks. Are you all set for the start of the semester tomorrow?"

"Looking forward to it. I like the environment at Davis. I've especially enjoyed the department chair and a few others who were teaching during the summer. We should get some great discussions going." He smiled. "It's not as dull as you might think."

"I can picture you in a deep, passionate discussion with your peers. I can't picture it as boring, at all. Just way over my head."

Dylan burst through the door and headed straight for Marcy, giving her a big hug. "Have you seen it? What did you think?"

"I waited for you," she said, catching her breath. He'd become so much more open and gregarious it was hard to believe it was the same young man as the one she'd met five weeks ago, looking starved and desperate.

"Awesome! Thanks. Come on!" He tugged on her hand, pulling her out of the chair and to the kitchen.

Marcy had expected good. She hadn't expected out-of-this-world good. In one sense it was so suited to the house, it seemed original to it. But the glass upper cabinets and stainless-steel appliances brought it current, too.

"This is gorgeous," she said, awed. "Spectacular." Then she noticed some things in particular. She turned to look at Eric, who smiled softly. "You incorporated my ideas."

"We all thought they made sense." He opened the pantry door, showing off the additional storage space. Then she moved to the granite-topped peninsula, with plenty of counter space for prep work—and a view of the backyard.

Tears welled in her eyes, which was so stupid. It wasn't her kitchen, but she felt pride of ownership of it.

"Geez, Marcy, you don't need to get all emotional about a kitchen," Dylan said, his gaze shifting to Eric, who came up and put an arm around her.

"You really are exhausted. I think you should lie down for a while."

She nodded, unable to come up with a refusal that wouldn't make her seem silly. "Just for a little while," she said. "Wake me up in an hour."

Eric climbed the stairs with her, held the sheet up as she toed off her sandals then got into bed. He closed the blinds. By the time he'd returned to her, she'd fallen asleep. He brushed her hair from her face, kissed her forehead and left the room quietly.

"She had a long, busy week," he said to a worried-looking Dylan.

"It's scary," Dylan said. "Seeing her like that. She's usually got more energy than me and you together."

Eric had thought the same thing.

"Are you going to wake her up in an hour?" Dylan asked.

"Maybe in two. She'd be pretty ticked if I let it go longer than that."

Dylan grinned. "Yeah. She was pretty impressed, don't you think?"

Eric glanced around the room, nodding. "The yard's looking good, too. You've worked your tail off."

"Thanks."

Eric leaned against the counter. "What now, Dylan?"

"I don't want to move home." The answer came out fast and sure.

Eric was way too happy about that—and couldn't show it. "Why not?"

"It would be like taking a step back, don't you think? I need to do this on my own."

"Do what?"

"Grow up. Be responsible."

"You're eighteen, not twenty-five. You're entitled to some help."

"I know. And I'll take some help. I'm not stupid." He grinned. "But moving home isn't help. It would make things easier in a way, but I don't think *easy* is the way I want to go. Your lectures have paid off, I guess."

"Did I lecture?"

He shrugged, but there was humor in his eyes. "Don't get me wrong. I appreciate the advice and examples, even if I don't show it. It sunk in."

Eric had been proud of the way his brothers and sister had turned out, and he was just as proud about Dylan. He was a remarkable young man who would be successful at whatever he chose to do.

Eric pulled the teenager into a hug. They slapped each other's backs then let go, a little embarrassed.

"I think we should barbecue hamburgers when Marcy wakes up," Eric said.

"Good plan."

The emotional moment had passed, each of them saying something important to each other without using words. They prepped what they could for dinner then started a chess match. After two hours, Eric headed up to his room, saying to Dylan as he went, "You've got my back, right?"

Dylan's laughter followed Eric up the stairs and into the bedroom, where his sleeping beauty slumbered.

Marcy heard the bedroom door open, pulling her from a wild dream where she'd been running and running, over bridges and down trails that led nowhere. She struggled to slough off the dream as the room filled with light when Eric opened the blinds.

He sat on the bed and brushed her hair from her face and gave her a delicate kiss. "Better?" he asked.

"I'm not sure yet. Still a little groggy. What time is it?"

"Six-forty-five."

"You let me sleep too long."

"Shoot me."

She smiled. In fact, she was grateful for the extra rest.

"Dylan and I are fixing us all hamburgers."

"Yum." She struggled to sit up, was aware of how closely he watched her, like a bug under a microscope. "I'm fine, Eric. Really."

"Why are you pushing yourself so much? Working so hard?"

"It's rare that I have the kind of week I just had. I'll catch up." She laid a hand along his face, which he covered with his own. "Thank you."

"I think you need a keeper."

It was the wrong thing to say. She dropped her hand. "Don't patronize me. I've been taking care of myself for ten years, and doing a darned good job of it."

"I didn't mean it like—" He stopped. "You're right. I apologize."

What could she say to that? She hadn't even worked up a full head of steam yet and now it just fizzled. "I'll clean up and be down in a minute."

He kissed her, lightly at first, then with passion. "I'm looking forward to the one you owe me," he said against her lips.

"One-track mind."

"You bet." He leaned back. "This week sometime?"

"I'm staying with Lori and the kids this week. And Dylan will be here, so...."

He got up and left the room. She joined him in a few minutes. By the time she was ready to leave a few hours later, she'd eaten a hearty hamburger, helped him stow his kitchenware, and written down all the items he still needed, especially to throw a party.

He walked her to her car, then handed her an envelope filled with twenty-dollar bills. "For expenses."

She tucked it in her back pocket. "I'll be back on

Saturday to get things started, then Sunday morning to finish up."

"We'll be at Becca's on Saturday."

"I have the key you gave me."

"You know you can stay here instead of with your friend."

"I know. Thank you."

"But *no, thank you*."

She smiled. "Yes."

He fingered her hair. "Would you meet me at a hotel?"

Her entire body reacted to his touch and sexy tone of voice. "I could be convinced to do that," she said.

"This week?"

She laughed, but it wasn't really funny to her. This relationship had to end soon. Had to. It was becoming too hard not to tell him she loved him when she knew it wasn't what he needed. *She* wasn't what he needed. "You are the most persistent man I've ever met."

"Is that good?"

"It just *is.* Wednesday or Thursday. You choose."

"The sooner the better. I'm ready to collect."

She looked around. It was dark. She couldn't hear anyone nearby, so she kissed him. "I'm ready to pay. Good night, Professor."

He ran a finger down her nose. "Good night, Sleeping Beauty."

She thought about him calling her that all the way to Lori's apartment. No one had ever used a term of endearment with her. Oh, maybe a few times someone had called her babe, but that was something lots of people used.

Sweetheart. Now *that* would be an endearment.

Lori's boys were asleep when Marcy arrived, but Lori was watching television.

"Uh-oh," Lori said. "You've got that glow."

Marcy dropped onto the sofa beside her. "What glow is that?"

"The this-has-gone-beyond-a-fling glow."

All the more reason to wrap up the relationship, Marcy thought. "Maybe so, but don't fret about it. He doesn't have the same glow. In fact, he seems very happy in the fling mode."

"I'm not worried about him. He's a man. Men recover. I'm worried about you."

"I'm fine. I've got my eyes open, Lori. Truly." Her friend looked more than a little worried. "I will finish college, just like I promised you and my mom. I will have a career, a good one, before I have children. Nothing will change that. I'm one hundred percent committed." She snuggled into the couch pillows, knowing she couldn't go to bed until Lori did, when the couch would be empty. "So, what are we watching?"

Lori gave Marcy a pointed look. *"Dear John."*

She laughed. "I'm not quite ready to write that letter yet."

"You need to be thinking about it."

"I am. All the time." She considered the situation. "Not everyone ends up in your situation, Lor. There are some decent men out there who don't run away."

"I know that, Marcy. I do. I don't blame the entire gender, although I know it sounds like I do sometimes, because sometimes it's that anger that keeps me going. Otherwise I might fall totally apart. But we're not talking about other people, we're talking about you. You've seen firsthand what *can* happen."

Marcy was done with the discussion. She rested her feet on the coffee table and watched the rest of the movie with Lori. Marcy cried at the end, but Lori didn't. Had she become that hard-hearted that she couldn't be touched by sentimentality anymore?

Marcy didn't want to become hard like that. She wanted to keep her optimism and appreciation of life.

As she stretched out on the sofa to sleep, she remembered the way Eric had taken care of her. What was so wrong with letting a man do that now and then? It wasn't as if she couldn't take care of herself, after all. She'd done so for years. But sharing a load? That wasn't a bad thing, even if only temporary.

But wouldn't it be hard to go back to doing it alone?

It was the question she fell asleep thinking about.

Chapter Sixteen

The following Saturday at Becca and Gavin's house-warming party, Sam Sheridan leaned close to his brother Eric at the dinner table

"Becca's even happier now than at her wedding," Sam said.

Eric nodded. He'd noticed it, too. "And relaxed. She's been super-charged for so long that the change is noticeable, I think. Marriage is good for her. This small town is good for her, too."

"There's a softness about her."

Eric studied his sister. Their meal was over, but they were all lingering around the table—the siblings, Gavin and his parents, his sister Shana, Dylan, and Kincaid—the star of the moment for the beautiful renovation he'd done on the hundred-year-old house. Shana's daughter banged a toy on a high-chair tray and giggled.

"You're right, Sam," Eric said. "'Soft' is a good word for her. Her edges have dulled." He'd enjoyed spending time with his brothers again. A few months ago they'd also spoken about moving to Sacramento when Eric had made his decision to move there, but nothing had come of it, so Eric decided they'd been kidding around. His need for his family seemed to be escalating now that his own house was almost finished and he was established in his new position. He wanted to share his life, especially with those he loved most.

And he needed to create a family of his own. Wanted a wife and children. It'd been his number-one reason for moving across the country to a smaller city, for enjoying a slower pace.

Instead, what had he done? Gotten involved with a woman who had no interest in settling down. If only she—

Gavin stood and tapped his glass with a knife, drawing everyone's attention. He set down the knife so that he could take Becca's hand. "We want to thank all of you for coming, especially the Sheridan men, who flew thousands of miles to join us. Now that you see we have four extra bedrooms, we hope you'll come back often and hang out with us."

He lifted his glass in a toast. Everyone followed suit, whether they had beer, iced tea or soda. "And here's to Kincaid for taking on an enormous job and doing this great old gal justice."

Everyone took a sip. "And to Shana, who helped us create a home with her exquisite taste and bargain buys. No one decorates a house like you do, sis."

Which required another lifted glass and sips from everyone.

"And finally, Becca and I are happy to announce we're expecting a baby. The due date is April first, but it's no April Fools' joke."

Almost everyone was up on their feet instantly to offer hugs and handshakes. Eric almost couldn't stand. Becca was the youngest, the baby, and she was having the first child among them. Although since she was the only one married, that made sense, he reminded himself, getting up to congratulate the happy couple. There were hugs and handshakes, happy tears, playful comments about Gavin delivering his own baby when the time came. Chance City was small, and he was the only doctor in town.

"I hate to break into this celebration," Kincaid said, coming up beside Eric, "but I've got to leave, and I'd like to talk to you first."

"Sure. In private, you mean?"

"Here's fine. It's noisy enough that I don't think Dylan will hear, although I'll need to include him in a minute."

"All right," Eric said, intrigued.

"I want to offer Dylan a job. It'd mean moving here to Chance City, but it would be long term. Would you be okay with that? I won't ask him if you're not."

It was the second big blow in a ten-minute period. Becca was having a baby and Dylan could be moving out just when Eric had gotten comfortable having him around all the time. He had plans for Dylan, was going to approach him about his ideas this week, in fact.

"By all means, talk to Dylan," Eric said, feeling his world tilting a little but knowing it was the right thing to do. He gestured to the teenager to join them.

"Your brothers are great," Dylan said. "They're funny!"

"They are that. Um, Kincaid wants to ask you something."

Dylan looked at Kincaid expectantly. He looked so young, but also so ready to find his place in the world. "Shoot."

"First of all," Kincaid said, "I was really impressed by the work you did on Eric's kitchen. And I don't impress easily."

Dylan flashed a grin. "Thanks. You made it easy."

"You have talent. I know you've said you want to be an auto mechanic, but I'd like you to reconsider. You'd be a great carpenter. I've had a one-man business for a long time, and I've accepted jobs only when I wanted to. I'm thinking it's time to let it grow a little. So I'm offering you a job, full-time. It'll be more than forty hours a week, and you'll be bone-tired every night. I believe you'll not just be good at it, but find satisfaction in the work, too. Even when it rains, you'll be busy. I do a lot of interior work."

His expression serious, Dylan looked at Eric.

"And I'd planned on offering to send you to college or mechanic's school. So, now you have options to consider," Eric said.

"Think it over," Kincaid said. "I don't need an answer right now. Just so you know, the job includes a company truck. You'd have to live with me for a month or two at first probably."

"I don't even know what to say," Dylan said. "I—"

"Really, Dylan, I don't want an answer yet. Think about it. Talk it over with Eric. I'll be coming to your housewarming tomorrow. You can tell me then—or next week." He pulled out his cell phone and looked at it. "There's somewhere I need to be right now, so I don't even have time to discuss it further, anyway."

They shook hands, then Kincaid said his goodbyes to Becca and Gavin before he left.

"That came out of the blue," Dylan said.

"Sometimes the best opportunities do," Eric said. "What's your gut reaction?"

"To take him up on it." He looked a little sheepish. "I'd decided to become a mechanic because I knew I'd be good at it, but also because it was different from what my dad did. But I sure felt at home working on your kitchen."

"You looked it, too. And Kincaid praised you enough to confirm it." Eric could feel Dylan moving on already, his thoughts focused on the excitement of something new. "Kincaid's right. You'd be a great carpenter. And you'd be working with the best. I gather he created this life for himself. He emancipated himself at sixteen, moved here and built a small empire. He doesn't own just a few rental properties, as he put it, but a lot of them. What he doesn't own he's renovated and sold for profit. No reason why you couldn't do the same, especially since he's already well established. There'd be no struggle to find work."

"I guess that doesn't leave me with much of a decision, does it?" Dylan scratched his head and smiled a little.

"You could at least pretend to think about it."

Dylan looked horrified that he'd offended Eric.

Eric smiled. "Take until tomorrow, at least, anyway. Tell him in person."

"It's time for family photos," Becca called.

They posed for pictures in many different configurations and combinations, until someone finally yelled "Uncle!" and ended it.

A little later, his brothers and Dylan got into Eric's car and headed back to Davis. Maybe it seemed a little strange to be gathering most of the same group tomorrow at his own housewarming, but the Sheridan family probably wouldn't get together as one again until Christmas. They needed to celebrate now. If they waited, the excitement and newness of the new house would be anticlimactic, and a housewarming unimportant.

He wondered if Marcy was still there, setting up and prepping. He wasn't sure he wanted her to be. Their night in the hotel on Wednesday had whetted his appetite for more, not diminished it. He kept waiting for it to even out, but it escalated every day, whether or not he saw her.

But Becca's announcement had acted like a bucket of ice water dumped over him.

Dylan's life decisions had ended up being nobrainers. Kincaid's offer was the right choice for him.

Eric's, however, broke into two paths, neither easy. There was Marcy, sexy Marcy, who didn't want what he wanted. And he didn't think he could wait any longer for what awaited him on the other path, a wife and family. Not now. Not at this age.

If only he could merge the paths into one…

Marcy unboxed the new coffee maker and toaster, having convinced Eric that the new kitchen required new appliances. She'd also found a gorgeous ceramic fruit bowl for the kitchen table, handmade canisters for the countertop and a few brightly colored dish towels to bring vibrancy to the space.

She set out dishes and silverware, planned where each dish for the buffet would sit on the peninsula, then she prepared a couple of dishes that needed to refrigerate overnight, a roasted artichoke salad and a pasta salad. In a plastic bag, she marinated a tri-tip roast to barbecue. In the morning she would pick up cheese trays, slice baguettes and make a big fruit salad.

A large metal bucket would be filled with ice to nestle drinks into.

Item after item was ticked off her master list, until there was nothing more she could do until tomorrow.

And she was exhausted. She didn't understand why. She was caught up on sleep, at least as much as she usually got in a week. The past few days she'd felt like she was coming down with the flu, but was better by noon, except for dragging through the rest of the day. She'd been burning the candle at both ends for weeks, and now she must be paying for it.

She heard Eric's car pull into the driveway. If only they'd come five minutes later, she would've been gone. But she put on her best smile to meet his brothers, Sam, Trent and Jeff. Obviously they shared DNA—all of them tall, athletic and attractive—but each was individual, too. Dylan seemed to adore them. He was on a high like she hadn't seen.

"How was the party?" she asked, inching toward the front door to take off.

"Gavin and Becca announced that she's pregnant," Eric said. "And Dylan was offered a job working for Kincaid. Looks like he'll be moving out tomorrow."

She studied Eric's face and saw emotion there, but she couldn't put a name to it.

"Can you believe it?" Dylan asked, giving her a hug, then telling her the details of the job as the brothers— except Eric, who disappeared into the kitchen—made themselves at home, turning on the television and finding a ball game.

"I can believe it, Dylan. I'm so happy for you."

"It never would've happened without you and Eric. I told him I'd redo his bathrooms for free when he's ready."

And you get a little more experience under your belt, she thought. She didn't want to bring down his excitement one iota, nor his sense of being able to do anything. She remembered at eighteen feeling that way, too.

"I need to get to Score," she said. "I'll see you tomorrow. We'll celebrate more then."

She told the brothers it was nice meeting them, then went in search of Eric to say goodbye. He was seated on the back deck, in the shade. He didn't even look her way when she came through the door.

Marcy could hear Annie and Lucy playing next door. "Have you seen much of Annie?" she asked.

"No."

"Why not?"

He gave her an odd look. "There's nothing there, okay? Annie and I talked about it. I don't know what you think you saw, but it wasn't attraction, on either of our sides."

Marcy sat on the lounge, facing him. "I apologize." She didn't think that was why he was upset, however, so she pushed a little. "So, you've done your job well, and Dylan's on his way," she said.

"Looks like it."

"It's making you sad?"

He shrugged. "I've gotten used to him being around."

More than that, Marcy thought. He'd become like a father to the teenager, now he had to give him wings. Every parent probably struggled with that.

She laid a hand on his. He let it lie there, didn't hold hers in return, so she pulled it back.

"Is Becca feeling okay?" she asked, worried about how distant he was.

"She says she has morning sickness and is tired most of the time, but otherwise yes, everything is going fine. She's due April first. I've never seen her so happy and content."

"Are you upset about Dylan or is your sister's pregnancy troubling you somehow?"

He squinted, looking straight ahead. "Both, I think."

"I understand about Dylan, but Becca? I don't get it."

He finally looked her in the eye. "I want what she has, Marcy. You know that."

"And I'm in the way," she said quietly, a lump forming in her throat. "You're too honorable to seek out someone to marry and grow old with as long as I'm in the picture."

"I don't know what to do."

"I can make it easy for you, Eric." It was hard to say the words, but she'd known all along they would need saying at some point. "I can go away. Leave you free to get on with your life. It's going to end sometime. Maybe now *is* the time."

"Maybe you're right."

Devastated that he'd agreed, she struggled to breathe.

The back door burst open. Sam leaned out to say, "Hey, bro, your alma mater's playing on TV. Fourth quarter, all tied up. Oh, sorry. I didn't mean to intrude."

"It's fine," Marcy said, standing, shaking. "I have to get to work. I'll see you tomorrow morning. Bye."

He didn't try to stop her. Didn't say her name. Didn't follow her.

It wasn't until halfway through her shift at Score that Eric's words about Becca sank in: "She has morning sickness and is tired most of the time...."

Marcy ducked into the kitchen to look at the calendar. They'd used protection, except the first time. She had been sure she hadn't been ovulating that day. Positive of it.

Maybe she was wrong. She hadn't had a period since then, she realized, only some spotting, which wasn't usual for her. Her breasts had been tender, but they sometimes got tender right before her period. She'd had too much else on her mind to put two and two together.

She was on autopilot for the rest of the shift, then stopped at an all-night store to pick up a pregnancy test. Lori's apartment was quiet when she got there. She went straight to the bathroom. Her hand shook as she administered the test.

Then she waited and waited, her stomach roiling, nausea threatening.

When the time was up she looked.

Positive.

She and Eric were going to have a baby, the very situation she'd promised herself she wouldn't ever be in.

It was exactly what he wanted—although not with her. And she wanted him, but not this way. Not because she was pregnant. And not when she hadn't fulfilled her promise to Lori and, more importantly, to herself.

Now neither she nor Eric had a choice.

Chapter Seventeen

All the signs that the housewarming party was a success were visible—guests mingling and talking, food being consumed and raved about, and no one seemed to be in a hurry to leave, although Marcy knew the Sheridan brothers needed to take off for the airport soon. Which meant that everyone else would go, too, including Kincaid, who would take Dylan home with him. The finality of that was huge to her, so she could only imagine how Eric felt.

She'd offered to stay and clean up while he drove his brothers to the airport. She needed time to talk in private, needed to tell him she was pregnant. Even though yesterday he'd wanted to end their relationship.

She hadn't shared her news with Lori this morning for two reasons. Eric needed to be the first to know, and Lori would've offered her opinion, one which Marcy probably didn't want to hear. Whatever happened, it would be Eric and Marcy's decision alone.

Shana waved a hand in front of Marcy's face. "Calling all hired wives," she said, grinning. She carried her sweet Emma on her hip. At fourteen months, she was walking but not talking a whole lot.

Marcy gave Emma a cracker, and she smiled sweetly. "Sorry, Shana. I've been pretty distracted all day." How she'd even focused enough to do everything amazed even her. Thank goodness for lists.

"Well, the party is a huge success, so you can relax. And two of Eric's coworkers asked me for my business card, so I couldn't be happier. Good thing I had some printed up."

"Maybe you won't be working for At Your Service much longer," Marcy said.

"I wish that were true, but it'll be a long time until I'm able to support Emma and myself on interior-design work alone. Takes forever to get established since it's mostly word of mouth, but I'll get there. I wish I'd figured out it was what I'd wanted to do years ago and started training for it. Would've made life for Emma and me a whole lot easier." She kissed her daughter's forehead. "We've struggled unbelievably. Without my sister, Dixie, and my brother... Well, really, without Dixie's mother-in-law, Aggie, too, I'm not sure we would've survived at all."

"What about your parents?"

She shrugged. "There are difficulties there. I'm working on them."

"Have you always been a single mom?"

"Yes. Her daddy died before we knew I was pregnant. Before we could get married, even, although we'd been together for years."

"Oh, how sad that he never knew."

"My biggest regret." She nestled Emma close for a second. "It's a long story, Marcy, and I'd be happy to share. Maybe we could meet for lunch sometime? I work in Sacramento a lot."

"I'd like that."

Shana cocked her head. "I really admire you. You're setting yourself up for life before you have children. It's so much easier that way. Not that I'd change anything about having Emma.... Oh! Gavin's waving at me, saying it's time to go. I imagine everyone will be taking off."

A lot of hugging happened, then most of the party guests were gone. The brothers went outside, along with Kincaid, giving Eric and Marcy privacy to say goodbye to Dylan. He'd already loaded his belongings in Kincaid's truck.

He hugged Marcy first. Tears burned her eyes and throat. "I'm proud of you," she said. "Happy for you."

"Thanks. And thanks for everything you did. I'll never forget it."

"Stay in touch, okay?"

"I will." He turned to Eric. They just stared at each other.

Marcy thought she should probably leave them alone, but stood transfixed by the emotion passing between them.

"I'll do you proud," Dylan said.

"I know you will."

"And someday I'll help someone like you did me. I'll pay it forward."

"Can't ask for more than that." Eric wrapped his arms around Dylan and pulled him close. Marcy saw Eric squeeze his eyes shut.

"I love you, man," Dylan said into Eric's shoulder, and then he pushed away and ran out of the house.

Eric stared, swallowed, blew out a shaky breath. He finally looked at Marcy, his eyes gone dull. "Will you be here when I get back?"

"Yes."

He ran a hand down her hair, then off he went, too, and she was left alone to clean up and wait for what would probably be the longest hour of her life.

Eric knew he needed to finish the conversation he and Marcy had started yesterday, but he wished they didn't have to be civil, that they could just go upstairs to his bedroom, make love and then spend the night in each other's arms. He needed that. Needed her. Not conversation, civil or otherwise.

He'd like to tell her how he really felt, just be honest about everything, but he figured it would hurt her too much. He didn't want to hurt her, even though it meant he'd be left hurting just as much.

He found her curled up on the living-room sofa, the music turned on soft and low. She'd worked hard to make his party a success. After serving at Score last night, she couldn't have gotten more than a few hours' sleep. And she'd started off last night exhausted.

"Hi," she said, blinking a few times. "Guess I dozed off."

"I guess you needed it." He sat beside her. "Thank you. Everyone had a good time."

"You're welcome. It was my pleasure, really. I enjoyed all of it. Your new kitchen is a cook's dream."

"We're stalling," he said after a few seconds passed.

"You first," she said, looking a little haunted.

"Okay. Right before you left yesterday, you offered to go away."

"And you agreed."

"I said *maybe* you were right. I spent a lot of sleepless hours thinking about it. You." He took her hand. "I'm not ready to let go of you. And as you noted once, I can't sleep with you and date someone else. It's not who I am."

"I don't know what that all means."

"It means that I want to take this relationship to whatever end there is, whether I decide to end it or you do. Until then, it's just you and me."

"Even though I'm not the one you want."

He frowned. "I want you. I think I've shown that at every possible opportunity."

"I don't mean *want* in the physical sense, but the permanent sense."

"You mean, like marriage? You're the one who says I'm too old and settled, and you've got miles to go before you sleep."

She looked at her lap. "Well, sometimes people change their minds."

Hope stampeded inside of him. "Have you changed yours?"

She lifted her head and met his gaze. "I'm pregnant."

Aside from feeling punched in the stomach, the logistics struck him first. "We used protection every time. Except…"

"The first time, yes."

"Which you were sure, *positive,* was safe."

"I *was* sure. My body wasn't, I guess. Believe me, I'm struggling over this, too, Eric. But I am twenty-nine days pregnant."

Suddenly all the who, what, why, when, where and hows scattered into oblivion. Nothing mattered but the fact she was pregnant. She would never leave. He was going to be a father. He'd been given the opportunity he'd been wishing for and knew, for her sake, he couldn't admit, even to himself.

"We'll get married right away," he said. "We can go to Tahoe. I wish you'd told me earlier. My brothers could've stayed. I—"

"Slow down," she said.

He clamped his mouth shut.

"You are an honorable man, and I know to you there are no options other than getting married right away."

"You're right, Marcy. There are none."

He'd closed up. She could see that clearly. This wouldn't be teamwork, not this time. "I think we owe it to ourselves to take a few breaths, to get used to the idea. And maybe to figure out how to make a marriage work without love." There. She'd said it. "Marriage is hard enough when you love each other. And women often end up alone and struggling to make ends meet. Again, I know you're an honorable man, Eric, but the reason why I need to finish college and establish a career is because of all those women who also thought they were marrying honorable men, then found out otherwise."

His jaw went rigid. "Wait here."

He raced upstairs and came down with his laptop,

set it on his lap and typed in letters and numbers. Finally he turned it so that she could see the screen.

"Check the bottom line. That's my net worth. I'll sign a prenup, if you need that security, but whatever happens, you won't have to struggle like Lori or Shana. Or Annie. Or any other single mom you know. But even more important, Marcy, I would never leave you."

"But you could die! Look at Annie." The thought of him not being in her life slammed into her, stealing her breath.

"And no amount of money will stop that kind of pain," he said, putting an arm around her. "But you would have enough to have choices. Conveniences. Security. That makes me feel good."

She understood his need to prove he could provide well. He probably already had more than they could use in a lifetime. "You could've bought a mansion, many mansions. Why did you buy a foreclosure that needed so much work?"

"I liked the house and the neighborhood. I want a normal, regular life. I made a lot of money by creating my own hedge fund. Once I had enough saved up, I shut it down. Now I just manage my investments. I don't have to work, either, but I love what I do." He held her gaze. "So, now that those issues are out of the way, what else?"

"College," she said. "Career."

"Marcy," he said tenderly, patiently. "You're not seeing the forest for the trees, sweetheart."

Sweetheart. He'd called her sweetheart. "In what way?"

"You are so good at taking care of people, why would you get a business degree, of all things?"

"Because I want a good career." She was running out of steam and reasons to defend her plan. He'd just taken away one of the big reasons she'd been on this path to start with.

"I get that you want a career," he said as if amazed himself. "I finally see that. I think I've been angry at my mother all these years, because it was the fact she was working that led to the accident that killed her and my father. I needed something to blame. I blamed her having a career."

She wrapped her hand around his and squeezed.

"Continue on with college after the baby comes, if that's what you want. I'll support you one hundred percent, through school and a career, or whatever it is you want," he said. "But please choose something that makes sense for you, even if it's the job of stay-at-home mom. You'd be great at it. At least consider it as an option. You could make significant contributions in the volunteer world as well as right here. And by the time the kids are in school or gone from the nest, you might want to do something entirely different. You have the luxury of choices."

She put her hand over her mouth as she started to cry. It was her secret wish. Her deep-seated, forever-secret wish. She'd tried to be so practical for so long, when what she'd wanted all along was exactly what he was offering.

Except for one thing. "What about love?" she asked, almost choking on the question.

"I'm hopeful that love will happen. I think we have most of the requirements already. We're really good friends, and we can't keep our hands off each other—

solid places to start, don't you think? I promise I'll do my best to—"

Love you. Those were the words she expected, but he actually said, "I promise I'll do my best to win your love."

She felt her mouth drop open. "Are you saying you love me?"

He gave her a long look. "I sent you lavender roses, Marcy. I can't believe you didn't look up the meaning."

"I did. I couldn't imagine you knowing their meaning, however."

"I'm very thorough." He wiggled his eyebrows, and she laughed. "Of course I love you. I loved you at first sight. Maybe it took me a little longer than first sight to see it clearly, but looking back, I know it happened that very first night."

"I love you, too. I have for a long time."

He touched foreheads with her. "And here we thought we were being so honest with each other. Why didn't you tell me?"

"Because I knew you wanted a wife and children, and I didn't think I was ready yet. When I discovered last night I was pregnant, all the lies I'd told myself or been convinced of faded away. I knew you would marry me, but I didn't know it would be for all the right reasons."

His laughter filled the room with joy. She felt loved and cherished and very, very lucky. If one small thing hadn't happened the way it had along the way, they wouldn't have found each other.

He scooped her up and whirled her around until she stopped him. "Delicate stomach, you know?"

"Sorry. I'm happy, Marcy. So incredibly happy. We

never have to spend another night apart." He frowned a little. "You can get out of the house-sitting jobs, can't you? Will you?"

"I can and will. There are people clamoring for those jobs."

"This house has been yours all along. You put your stamp on it every day." He cupped her face. "That first night, I realized you'd already turned it into a home for me, even provided me with a child—Dylan. Then the moment he left, you provided another. Maybe a little girl with hazel eyes and curly auburn hair. How fast can you put a wedding together?"

"So fast it'll make your head spin. In the meantime, I think I can come up with a few ways to distract you while you wait, Professor."

Then even though it was only eight o'clock, they turned out the lights, closed the blinds and climbed the stairs to their bedroom where she distracted him completely and cherished him and adored him, doing what she did best, taking care of him.

And the more she gave, the more she got. She was the happiest woman on earth.

* * * * *

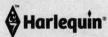
Harlequin®

*Harlequin Romantic Suspense presents the latest book
in the scorching new* KELLEY LEGACY *miniseries
from best-loved veteran series author Carla Cassidy*

*Scandal is the name of the game as the Kelley family fights
to preserve their legacy, their hearts…and their lives.*

Read on for an excerpt from the fourth title
RANCHER UNDER COVER

*Available October 2011
from Harlequin Romantic Suspense*

"**W**ould you like a drink?" Caitlin asked as she walked
to the minibar in the corner of the room. She felt as if she
needed to chug a beer or two for courage.

"No, thanks. I'm not much of a drinking man," he
replied.

She raised an eyebrow and looked at him curiously as she
poured herself a glass of wine. "A ranch hand who doesn't
enjoy a drink? I think maybe that's a first."

He smiled easily. "There was a six-month period in my
life when I drank too much. I pulled myself out of the bottom of a bottle a little over seven years ago and I've never
looked back."

"That's admirable, to know you have a problem and then
fix it."

Those broad shoulders of his moved up and down in
an easy shrug. "I don't know how admirable it was, all I
knew at the time was that I had a choice to make between
living and dying and I decided living was definitely more
appealing."

She wanted to ask him what had happened preceding
that six-month period that had plunged him into the bottom

of the bottle, but she didn't want to know too much about him. Personal information might produce a false sense of intimacy that she didn't need, didn't want in her life.

"Please, sit down," she said, and gestured him to the table. She had never felt so on edge, so awkward in her life.

"After you," he replied.

She was aware of his gaze intensely focused on her as she rounded the table and sat in the chair, and she wanted to tell him to stop looking at her as if she were a delectable dessert he intended to savor later.

Watch Caitlin and Rhett's sensual saga unfold amidst the shocking, ripped-from-the-headlines drama of the Kelley Legacy miniseries in

RANCHER UNDER COVER

Available October 2011 only from Harlequin Romantic Suspense, wherever books are sold.

Harlequin® SHOWCASE 2 1 GREAT NOVELS GREAT PRICE

USA TODAY Bestselling Author

RaeAnne Thayne

**On the sun-swept sands of
Cannon Beach, Oregon, two couples
with guarded hearts search for
a second chance at love.**

Discover two classic stories of love and family
from the Women of Brambleberry House miniseries
in one incredible volume.

BRAMBLEBERRY SHORES

Available September 27, 2011.

www.Harlequin.com

HSC68836